1861–1941.

RABINDRANATH TAGORE

QUARTET
(CHATURANGA)

Translated from the Bengali by
Kaiser Haq

T0204523

HEINEMANN

Heinemann Educational Publishers
A Division of Heinemann Publishers (Oxford) Ltd
Halley Court, Jordan Hill, Oxford OX2 8EJ

Heinemann: A Division of Reed Publishing (USA) Inc.
361 Hanover Street, Portsmouth, New Hampshire, 03801–3912, USA

Heinemann Educational Books (Nigeria) Ltd
PMB 5205, Ibadan
Heinemann Educational Boleswa
PO Box 10103, Village Post Office, Gaborone, Botswana

FLORENCE   PRAGUE   PARIS   MADRID
ATHENS   MELBOURNE   JOHANNESBURG
AUCKLAND   SINGAPORE   TOKYO
CHICAGO   SAO PAULO

First published as *Chaturanga* in 1916
This translation © Kaiser Haq 1993
First published by Heinemann Educational in 1993

Series Editor: Ranjana Sidhanta Ash

British Library Cataloguing in Publication Data
A catalogue record for this book is available from the British Library.

Cover design by Touchpaper
Cover illustration by Matilda Harrison

ISBN 0435 95086 X

Phottypeset by Wilmaset Ltd, Birkenhead, Wirral
Printed and bound in Great Britain
by Cox & Wyman Ltd, Reading, Berkshire

94 95 10 9 8 7 6 5 4 3

PK
1723
.C4
E5
1993

SEP 12 1996

CONTENTS

Introduction to the Asian Writers Series

Heinemann's new Asian Writers Series, aided by the Arts
Council of Great Britain, intends to introduce English language
readers to some of the interesting fiction written in languages
that most will neither know nor study.

For too long popular acclaim for Asian writing in the West
has been confined to the handful of authors who choose to write
in English rather than in the language of their own cultures.
Heinemann's entry into the field should dispel this narrow
perspective and place modern Asian writing within the broad
spectrum of contemporary world literature.

The first six works selected for the series are translations of
novels from five languages: Bengali, Hindi, Malayalam, Tamil
and Urdu. The six novels span seventy-five years of change in
the subcontinent. *Quartet*, one of Rabindranath Tagore's most
skilfully constructed and lively classics, was first published in
1916, whereas the most recent work chosen, *The Fire Sacrifice*,
was written by the up-and-coming Hindi novelist Susham Bedi
and first published in 1989.

These first six titles face the normal problems affecting
literature in translation, not least the difficulty of establishing
an exact parallel of the thought or verbal utterance of the
original in the target language. When the source text is in a
non-European language and embodies a culture and literary
style quite alien to English language readers, the translator's
task is made even more difficult.

Susan Bassnett in her invaluable work on translation studies
describes the typical colonial attitude to the literature of the

colonised as a 'master and servant' relationship, with the European translator attempting to 'improve' and 'civilise' the source text. At the other end of the scale she describes a kind of 'cannibalism' in which the translator almost 'devours' the text to disgorge a totally new product. Fortunately, the translators of this series fall into neither category but manage to retain a balanced view of their craft.

While it is very important to produce a translation that uses a style both readable and engaging to an English language readership, it must not obscure the particularities of literary devices, figures of speech, and aesthetic detail that the author uses to convey his or her sensibility, imagination and verbal artistry. Should such faithfulness to the original produce in the English version a greater degree of sentiment or charged imagery than the reader might expect, one hopes that he or she will be ready to accept the novelty of writing from an unfamiliar source.

In publishing the Asian Writers Series, Heinemann is taking a bold step into an area which has been neglected for too long. It is our hope that readers will respond with interest and enthusiasm as they discover the outstanding quality of these novels.

RANJANA SIDHANTA ASH, SERIES EDITOR, 1993

Introduction to Quartet

Quartet (*Chaturanga* in the original Bengali) is one of the greatest novellas in world literature. The economy and concentration demanded by the form are perfectly exemplified in this tale of archetypal conflict – between reason and emotion, orthodoxy and liberalism, spiritual aspiration and earthy passion – set against the background of *fin-de-siècle* Bengal. That it is virtually unknown outside the native Bengal of its author, Rabindranath Tagore (1861–1941), and even there isn't one of his best-known works, is a lamentable instance of recognition deferred. However, a few discerning critics have long believed that it is artistically more satisfying than Tagore's longer and more celebrated novels; it more than makes up in intensity for what it lacks in detail, and is unique in the author's *oeuvre* for its range of technical experiments. Transitions in plot and character development are abrupt, descriptions are compressed into minimalist dimensions, the terse language flashes suddenly into image and epigram. Such devices have become part of the inherited repertoire of the contemporary writer, but if we remember that before book publication in 1916 *Quartet* was serialised in 1914–15, when literary modernism was still in its infancy, we will better appreciate its daring originality.

By the time Tagore came to write *Quartet* he had single-handedly transformed a fledgling tradition into what was then perhaps the most vital non-western literature, an achievement for which his 1913 Nobel Prize, following on the publication of his English translation of *Gitanjali*, was a fitting tribute. The Bengali language has a thousand years' history, but the sea-change wrought by western influence in the nineteenth century produced a new literature markedly different in form and sensibility from the region's folk poetry as well as the more self-conscious poetry produced under the patronage of its feudal potentates. Perhaps the most conspicuous product of the change was the birth of prose literature, which had previously existed only in a rudimentary form. Michael Madhusudan Dutt (1824–73) in poetry and drama, and Bankimchandra Chatterji (1838–94) in fiction, were the great nineteenth-century masters of the new literature. Tagore rapidly surpassed his predecessors and demonstrated such varied abilities and interests that Albert Schweitzer dubbed him 'the Indian Goethe'. In all he published – if I've got the count right – fifty-one volumes of poetry, ninety-five short stories, forty collections of essays, fifty-two plays, six travel books, twelve volumes of letters, fourteen novels and novellas. He also wrote over two thousand songs, set them to music and sang them. He produced his own plays and acted in them. Taking to art with sudden enthusiasm in his mid-sixties he turned out over three thousand paintings and drawings and came to be acknowledged the greatest Indian artist of this century. His life and art are informed by a coherent system of ideas with ramifications into philosophy and religion, socio-political theory, education theory and aesthetics. He studied and practised homoeopathic medicine, managed large ancestral estates, and set up the 'world university' of Visvabharati.

Following the award of the Nobel Prize, Tagore was widely translated into European languages and revered as a poet–guru. Then he was forgotten. He had gained fame as a mystic and visionary, and now these roles were no longer thought fitting for a serious writer. But there are other sides to Tagore that should win him a new readership. More than his poetry, which even in the best translations loses the charm of the original, it is his prose, if well translated, that will appeal to the world at large. In his non-fictional prose he is a brilliant essayist and a thinker of continuing relevance, while his fiction provides the finest portrait of Bengali society from the late nineteenth century to the thirties of this century.

In *Quartet*, the narrator, Sribilash, and his friend Sachish evolve with the dramatic unfolding of conflicts between western atheistic humanism and orthodox Hinduism, between humanism and Indian devotional cults, between mysticism and the demands of the life-force. Sachish's uncle, Jagmohan, is a staunch atheist, humanist and Utilitarian. Such personages were a lively presence in Calcutta in the second and third quarters of the nineteenth century. In his autobiography, *My Reminiscences*, Tagore records his boyhood experience under the tutorship of one of these iconoclasts: the pupil frequently suffered the mortification of being worsted in argument. The tables are turned in *Quartet*, where the atheist Jagmohan is at his creator's mercy. But, significantly, he is treated with a charming mixture of mild irony and sympathy. The Tagores were prominent members of the monotheistic Brahmo Samaj, a sect which opposed both idolatrous ritualism and ecstatic cults. It is therefore hardly surprising that the lash of unmitigated condemnation is reserved for Harimohan and his eldest son, who in their greed and hypocritical piety embody all that is wrong with traditional Hindu society, and for the dubious guru, Lilananda-swami (the 'Swami' is an honorific, often put separately before the name, as I have done in my translation to make it easier for the non-Indian reader to pronounce the whole).

Sachish starts off as a clone of Jagmohan, but the shock of the latter's death drives him into the arms of Swami Lilananda. However incredible the conversion may appear, it is both psychologically and historically plausible. The psychoanalyst Sudhir Kakar explains in *The Inner World* (Delhi: OUP, 1978) that the Indian tendency to withdraw into mysticism (or, for that matter, into political extremism) has its source in an underdeveloped ego, which needs the buttress of stable family and caste relationships. When these supports are threatened one feels totally lost and is likely to accept irrational solutions to life's problems. In Sachish's case, ironically enough, caste, religion and parents are renounced without loss of equilibrium because his uncle takes their place. But Jagmohan's death leaves him an easy prey to the lure of a devotional cult. Historically, the Indian humanists underwent a crisis at the turn of the nineteenth century, when they found human problems to be not particularly amenable to a positivist approach. Many of them turned round like Sachish.

Atheist humanism, orthodox Hinduism, the cult of ecstasy, Sachish's independent venture into mysticism, all are ultimately rejected in *Quartet*. The author's deviation from linear narrative in the latter parts succeeds particularly well in capturing the story's rising emotional intensity, and in convincingly projecting his idea of the good life through a tender love-story. Sribilash, *un homme moyen sensuel* (perhaps it will be truer to say he wears the mask of one), and Damini, the life-force personified, unpretentiously fulfil their commitments to themselves, their kinsfolk, friends and fellow citizens. Perhaps it *is* hubris to attempt more. It is also a relief to be told in the 'Postscript' to the third section that in the end Sachish too returns to social work, but without the abrasive propagandising of the past.

Translating Tagore into a European language is a challenge, and *Quartet* is particularly challenging because of its experimental qualities. I have tried to be true to the sense and feel of the original while keeping in mind the question of readability. The transliterated Bengali words have been kept to a minimum, and the meanings of nearly all of them can be gauged from the context. For those interested, a glossary provides further elucidation.

A few words of acknowledgement will be in order. But for the encouragement of my friend William Radice this translation would not have gone beyond the stage of conception. I am grateful to him too for painstakingly going over the manuscript and making valuable suggestions for improvement. In grappling with certain words and concepts I have benefited from the counsel of friends and colleagues in Dhaka, particularly Mr Kashinath Roy, Dr Naren Biswas and Dr Ahmed Kamal. As always I owe a debt to my wife, Dipa, for cheering me on.

KAISER HAQ, DHAKA, 1993

Translator's dedication

In memoriam Borokaka

Uncle

I came up from the country and entered college in Calcutta. Sachish was studying for his BA then. We were roughly the same age.

In appearance Sachish gives the impression of a celestial being. His eyes glow; his long, slender fingers are like tongues of flame; the colour of his skin is more a luminescence than a colour. As soon as I set eyes on him I seemed to glimpse his inner self; and from that moment I loved him.

Amazingly, many of his classmates harboured deep resentment against him. The fact is, those who are like everyone else arouse no hatred unless there is a reason. But when a resplendent inner self pierces the grossness that envelops it, some, quite irrationally, extend it heartfelt adoration; others, just as irrationally, try heart and soul to insult it.

The students I boarded with realized that I secretly admired Sachish. This became such a thorn in their sides that they didn't let a single day pass without reviling him in my hearing. I knew that if sand gets in the eye rubbing makes things worse; it was best not to respond to unpleasant words. But one day such calumny was poured on Sachish's character that I couldn't keep quiet any more.

I was at a disadvantage because I hadn't yet got to know him. On the other hand some of my opponents came from his neighbourhood, others claimed some sort of distant kinship with him. 'It's absolutely true!' they declared with great vehemence; with even greater vehemence I declared that I didn't believe an iota of it. At which they all belligerently rolled up their sleeves and called me a very impertinent fellow.

Tears welled up as I lay in bed that night. Between classes the next day, I went up to Sachish as he reclined with a book on the shaded grass by the circular pond and without a word of introduction launched into an incoherent torrent of words. He closed his book and gazed at me for a while. Those who haven't seen his eyes can never understand what lies in their gaze.

'Those who slander others,' Sachish said, 'do so because they love slander, not because they love truth. It's pointless therefore to struggle to prove that a piece of slander is untrue.'

'But if they're lying . . .'

Sachish stopped me. 'But you see, they're not liars. There's a poor boy in our neighbourhood who has palsy and shakes in every limb. He can't do any work. One winter I gave him an expensive blanket. That day my servant Shibu indignantly complained to me that the illness was a pretence. Those who deny any virtue in me are like Shibu. They believe what they say. An expensive extra blanket has fallen to my lot and all the Shibus in the land have decided I have no right to it. I would find it embarrassing to quarrel with them over this.'

Without responding to that I asked, 'But they say you're an atheist – is it true?'

'Yes, I am an atheist,' Sachish said.

My face fell. I had argued violently with my fellow boarders that Sachish could not be an atheist.

Indeed I suffered two nasty shocks at the very outset of getting to know Sachish. As soon as I saw him I decided he was a Brahmin's son. After all, his face was like a god's image carved out of marble. I had heard that his family name was Mullick; a *kulin* Brahmin household in our village bore the same name. But I discovered that Sachish was of the goldsmiths' caste. Ours was a devout *kaystha* family – for the goldsmiths' caste we felt profound contempt. And as for being an atheist, I knew it to be a greater sin than murder, or even eating beef.

I stared speechless at Sachish's face. Still the same luminescence there – as if prayer-lamps were shining in his soul.

No one would have thought I would ever share a meal with one of the goldsmiths' caste and in my fanatical atheism outdo my guru. With time even this came to pass.

Wilkins was professor of literature at our college. His impressive learning was matched by his contempt for the students. To him teaching literature to Bengali boys in a colonial college was tantamount to menial labour; and so if he came across the word 'cat', even in the course of teaching Milton or Shakespeare, he would gloss it with the explanation, 'a quadruped of the feline species'. But Sachish was excused from taking down such notes. 'Sachish,' he would say, 'I'd like to compensate you for having to sit in this class. Come to my house – there you'll get back your taste for literature.'

The incensed students claimed that the sahib was fond of Sachish because Sachish was light-complexioned and had beguiled him by showing off his atheism. The more cunning students rallied together and went to the sahib to ask to borrow a book on positivism; he dismissed them, saying, 'You won't understand it.' The imputation that they were unfit even to be atheists merely increased their rage against atheism and against Sachish.

2

I have listed the aspects of belief and behaviour that provoked condemnation in Sachish's life. Some of these I came to know before my acquaintance with him, some after.

Jagmohan was Sachish's uncle. He was a celebrated atheist of those times. It would be an understatement to say he didn't believe in God; he believed in 'no-God'. A battleship commander's occupation has more to do with sinking ships than with navigation; similarly, Jagmohan's theological enterprise lay in torpedoing manifestations of faith wherever he got a chance. This is how he marshalled his arguments before a believer:

'If God exists, then my intelligence is his creation. My intelligence says there is no God. Therefore God says there is no God. Yet you contradict him to his face and say that God exists! Thirty-three billion godlings will twist your ears to make you atone for this blasphemy.'

Jagmohan had married when still a boy. His wife died in his youth, but he had read Malthus in the meantime. He never married again.

His younger brother Harimohan was Sachish's father. Harimohan's character was so strikingly antithetical to his elder brother's that if I write about it readers will mistake it for fiction. But it is Fiction that must be chary in order to seduce the reader. Since Truth is not under such constraints it doesn't balk at being strange. And so, just as dawn and dusk are opposed in Nature, human society doesn't lack instances of similar opposition between elder and younger brother.

Harimohan had been a sickly child. He had to be protected from harm by all sorts of amulets and charms; rites of exorcism; water sanctified by washing sadhus' matted locks; dust from prominent holy places; food-offerings to deities and the ambrosial water that has washed their feet; and above all, the blessings obtained from priests at great expense.

Harimohan's illnesses left him when he grew up, but the belief that he was very delicate persisted in the family. Nobody wished of him anything more than that he should just stay alive somehow. He didn't disappoint anyone in this regard and went on living quite satisfactorily. But he kept everyone on tenterhooks by pretending that his health was always on the verge of collapse. Taking advantage of the apprehensions roused by his father's early death, he appropriated the doting attentions of his mother and aunts. He was served his meals before anybody else; his diet was specially prepared; he had to work less than others, but was entitled to more rest. He never forgot that he was in the special care not only of his mother and aunts but of the gods as well. He extended deference, in proportion to the quantity of favours he might expect in return, not only to the gods but to worldly powers – he held such personages as the OC of the police station, rich neighbours, highly placed civil servants, newspaper editors, not to mention Brahmin priests, in awed reverence.

Jagmohan's apprehensions were of a contrary sort. He avoided the powerful, lest anyone suspect him of currying favour. A similar attitude underlay his defiance of the deity: he simply refused to bow before any power, be it earthly or divine.

In due course, that is to say well before due time, Harimohan's marriage took place. After three daughters and three sons came Sachish. Everyone said he bore a striking resemblance to his uncle. Jagmohan too became deeply attached to the child, as if it were his own son.

At first Harimohan was pleased at the thought of the advantages accruing from this. For Jagmohan had taken on responsibility for the boy's education, and he was well known for his exceptional mastery of English. In the opinion of some he was the Macaulay of Bengal, to others he was Bengal's Dr Johnson. He seemed to be encased within a shell made up of English books. Just as a line of pebbles shows the course of a mountain stream, the parts of the house where he spent his time could be recognized by the English books lining the walls from floor to ceiling.

Harimohan lavished his paternal affection on his eldest son, Purandar. He could never say no to Purandar's demands. His eyes always appeared to brim with sentimental tears for this son; he feared that Purandar would simply cease to live if thwarted in anything. Purandar's education came to nothing. He had married very early, and no one had managed to bind him to his marital vows. When his wife protested vigorously, her father-in-law turned on her angrily and declared that her nagging had driven his son to seek solace elsewhere.

Observing such goings-on, Jagmohan sought to protect Sachish from the hazards of paternal love by never letting him out of sight. It wasn't long before Sachish, still at a very early age, acquired a sound knowledge of English. But he didn't stop there. With his brain cells kindled by Mill and Bentham, his atheism began to glow like a torch.

Jagmohan behaved with Sachish as if he was of the same age. He considered reverence for age an empty convention that confirmed the human mind in its servitude. A young man who had married into the family wrote to him, addressing the letter in traditional style, 'To Your Auspicious Feet'. He replied with the following advice:

My Dear Naren

What it means to describe the feet as 'auspicious', I do not know; nor do you; it is therefore sheer nonsense. Then again, you have completely ignored me and addressed my feet instead. You ought to know that my feet are a part of my body and cannot be seen as separate from me as long as they are not severed. Further, they are neither hand nor ear; to make an appeal to them is sheer madness. Finally, your choice of the plural number over the dual with reference to my feet may express reverence, given that a certain quadruped is an object of devotion to you, but it bespeaks an ignorance of my zoological identity that should, I feel, be removed.

Things that others sweep under the carpet Jagmohan openly discussed with Sachish. If anyone complained about this he would say, 'If you want to get rid of hornets, break up their nest. In the same way, removing the embarrassment that attaches to certain topics dispels the cause of embarrassment. I am breaking the nest of embarrassment in Sachish's mind.'

3

Sachish completed his degree. Harimohan now mounted a campaign to rescue him from his uncle. But the fish had swallowed the bait and was caught on the hook. The more one tried to pull it free the more firmly attached it became. Harimohan's anger at this was directed more at his brother than at his son. He strewed the neighbourhood with colourful slander about him.

Harimohan wouldn't have minded if it was only a question of opinions and beliefs; even eating forbidden chicken was tolerable – it could be passed off as goat. But his brother and son had gone so far in their behaviour that nothing could cover it up. Let me narrate the event that gave most offence.

Service to humanity was an important aspect of Jagmohan's atheistic creed. The chief delight in such altruism lay in that it brought nothing save financial loss – no award or merit, no promise of baksheesh from any scripture – nor did it placate any irate deity. If anyone asked, 'What is there for you in the greatest good of the greatest number?' he would say, 'The greatest thing for me is that there's nothing in it for me.' He would say to Sachish: 'Remember, my boy, our pride in being atheists requires us to be morally impeccable. Because we don't obey anything we ought to have greater strength to be true to ourselves.'

Sachish was his chief disciple in seeking the greatest good of the greatest number. In their neighbourhood there were some hide-merchants' warehouses. The social work of uncle and nephew brought them into such intimacy with the Muslim tanners and traders that Harimohan's caste mark positively blazed, and threatened to turn his brain into an inferno. Knowing that invoking scripture would have the opposite of the desired effect, Harimohan complained instead that Jagmohan was misusing their patrimony. 'Let my expenses reach what you have spent on fat-bellied priests,' Jagmohan replied, 'then I will square accounts with you.'

One day Harimohan's household noticed that preparations were afoot for a huge feast in Jagmohan's part of the house. The cooks and attendants were all Muslim. Beside himself with rage, Harimohan summoned Sachish and said, 'I hear you will treat all your *chamar* friends to a feast here?'

'I would if I had the means,' Sachish replied, 'but I don't have any money. They're coming as Uncle's guests.'

Stomping about in fury, Purandar threatened, 'I'll see how they dare come to this house to eat.'

When Harimohan protested to his brother, Jagmohan told him, 'I don't say anything about your daily food-offerings to your gods. So why do you object to my making an offering to *my* gods?'

'Your gods?'

'Yes, my gods.'

'Have you become a Brahmo?'

'Brahmos accept a formless deity who is invisible to the eye. You accept idols who cannot be heard. We accept the living who can be seen and heard – it's impossible not to believe in them.'

'What, these Muslim *chamars* are your gods?'

'Yes, these Muslim *chamars* are my gods. You will notice that among all deities they are distinguished by a remarkable ability to polish off whatever eatables are placed before them. None of your gods can do that. I love to watch this miracle, so I have invited my gods into my home. If you weren't blind to true divinity you would be pleased at this.'

Purandar went up to his uncle, said many harsh things in a loud voice, and declared that he would do something really drastic that day.

'You monkey,' Jagmohan said with a laugh, 'you have only to lay a finger on my gods to see how potent they are. I won't have to do a thing.'

No matter how boastful he was, Purandar was in reality even more of a coward than his father. He was formidable only with those who spoiled him. He didn't dare enrage his Muslim neighbours. He went instead to Sachish and abused him. Sachish merely raised his exquisite eyes towards his elder brother and didn't utter a word. That day the feast was held undisturbed.

4

Harimohan girded his loins now for a campaign against his elder brother. Both of them derived their income from the trusteeship of ancestral property endowed as a religious trust. Harimohan filed a suit in the district court in which he claimed that being an atheist, Jagmohan was ineligible for the trusteeship. Respectable witnesses for the plaintiff were not lacking; virtually the entire neighbourhood was ready to testify.

There was no need to resort to pettifoggery. Jagmohan unequivocally stated in court that he didn't believe in gods and goddesses; didn't care for scriptural restrictions on diet; didn't know from which part of Brahma's anatomy the Muslims had originated; nor saw any objections to dining or mixing socially with them.

The judge found Jagmohan unworthy of the trusteeship. Jagmohan's lawyers assured him that the judgement would be overturned in the High Court. But Jagmohan said, 'I will not appeal. I cannot cheat a god, even one I do not believe in. Only those stupid enough to believe in a god can deceive him in good conscience.'

'How will you live?' friends asked.

'If I can't get food,' he said, 'I'll live on air.'

Harimohan had no wish to boast of his victory in the law suit. He was apprehensive that his brother might put a curse on him. But Purandar still smarted at having failed to turn the tanners out of the house. Now that it was quite obvious whose gods were more potent, he hired drummers who from dawn on shattered the neighbourhood with their din.

What's up?' said a friend who called on Jagmohan, ignorant of what had transpired.

'Today my god is being dunked in the water with great pomp, hence the music,' Jagmohan replied.

For two days Brahmins were feasted under Purandar's personal supervision. Everybody declared he was the glory of his family.

Following this, the family home in Calcutta was divided between the two brothers by a wall down the middle.

Harimohan had enough confidence in human nature to assume that everybody – no matter what he thought of religion – possessed a natural good sense when it came to practicalities like food and clothing and money. He fully expected his son to abandon the impoverished Jagmohan and, drawn by the aroma of food, slip into the gilded cage. But Sachish had evidently inherited neither the piety nor the worldly wisdom of his father. He remained with his uncle.

Jagmohan had become so accustomed to treating Sachish as one of his own that it didn't strike him as extraordinary when on the day the house was partitioned his nephew fell to his share.

But Harimohan knew his brother only too well. He spread the rumour that Jagmohan was scheming to secure his own livelihood by holding on to Sachish. He put on a look of injured innocence and tearfully complained to everyone, 'I am not heartless enough to deprive my elder brother of food and clothing. But I will never tolerate his diabolical effort to manipulate my son. Let me see how far his cunning goes.'

When friends carried word of these developments to Jagmohan he was stunned. He cursed his own stupidity for not having anticipated them. 'Goodbye, Sachish,' he said to his nephew.

Sachish realized that the anguish with which Jagmohan had bid him farewell forbade any remonstrance. He would now have to end an association that had lasted without interruption through the eighteen years of his life.

When Sachish put his box and bedding-roll on the roof of the hackney carriage and was driven off, Jagmohan went up to his room, bolted the door and collapsed on to the floor. Dusk fell, the old servant knocked to be let in so he could light the lamp, but there was no response.

The greatest good of the greatest number, indeed! The statistical calculations of science do not apply to the mysteries of human nature. The person who is a single unit in a census is beyond the reckoning of statistics in matters of the heart. Sachish could not be categorized in terms of statistical units – one, two, three . . . He rent Jagmohan's heart and pervaded his whole world.

It hadn't occurred to Jagmohan to ask Sachish why he had ordered a carriage and loaded his belongings into it. Instead of moving to his father's half of the house Sachish went to a boarding-house where a friend of his lived. At the thought that one's own son could turn into a total stranger Harimohan shed frequent tears. He *was* very tender-hearted!

Soon after the partitioning, Purandar, out of sheer bloody-mindedness, set up a permanent altar for idol-worship in his father's half of the house and danced for joy at the thought that each morning and evening the noise of the ritual cymbals and conch-shells was driving his uncle to distraction.

Sachish took up tutoring pupils privately, and Jagmohan became headmaster of a high school. Harimohan and Purandar embarked on a mission to rescue the children of respectable families from the clutches of the atheist pedagogue.

5

One day not long afterwards Sachish suddenly appeared in Jagmohan's upper-floor study. The custom of making obeisance, or *pranam*, being alien to them, Jagmohan embraced Sachish and offering him a seat on the bed, asked, 'What news?'

There was indeed some special news.

A widowed girl called Nonibala and her widowed mother had taken refuge in the house of a maternal uncle. She was safe as long as her mother was with her, but the old woman had died not long ago. The girl's cousins were scoundrels. One of their cronies lured Nonibala out of the house and seduced her. After some days he became prey to jealousy, suspected Noni of betraying him, and started heaping insults on her. All this was going on next door to the house where Sachish was employed as tutor to the children. Sachish wanted to rescue the wretched girl. But he had neither money, nor a place where he could take her; hence the visit to Uncle. By now the girl had become pregnant.

Jagmohan flew into a rage. If he could have laid hands on the seducer he would have instantly crushed the fellow's head! He wasn't the sort of person to deliberate calmly on such matters. 'Very well,' he declared. 'My library is empty. I'll put her up there.'

'The library!' Sachish exclaimed in surprise. 'But what about the books?'

During the time that Jagmohan had been looking for a job he supported himself by selling off his books. Those that remained could be easily accommodated in his bedroom.

'Fetch the girl straightaway,' Jagmohan said.

'I've already brought her,' Sachish replied. 'She's waiting downstairs.'

Jagmohan went down and saw the girl cringing like a little bundle of rags on the floor of the room by the staircase. He swept into the room like a gale and said in his deep voice, 'Come, my little mother. Why are you squatting in the dust?'

The girl buried her face in a corner of her sari and broke into sobs.

Tears didn't come easily to Jagmohan's eyes, but they brimmed over now.

'Sachish,' he said, 'the shame this girl has to bear today belongs equally to you and me. Who has forced such a burden on her?'

Then to her, '*Ma*, your shyness won't do before me. My schoolmates nicknamed me Jagai the Madcap. I am still the same madcap.'

So saying he unhesitatingly took the girl's two hands and drew her to her feet. Her sari slipped from her head. Such a young and tender face, free of the slightest taint of disgrace! She was lovely as a raintree blossom, and just as dust on a flower cannot destroy its essential purity, so the beauty of her sacred inner being had remained unbesmirched. Her dark eyes were fearful like those of a wounded gazelle, her lissom frame was constricted by a sense of shame, but her frank sorrow revealed no sign of stigma.

Jagmohan took Nonibala upstairs to his room and said, '*Ma*, look at the state of my room. The broom hasn't touched it in ages, everything's topsy-turvy, and as for me I eat at no fixed time. Now that you are here, my room will become neat and tidy again, and even Jagai the Madcap will be able to live like a human being.'

Nonibala hadn't known till this day what human beings could mean to each other. She hadn't known it even when her mother was alive, for her mother had come to see her not simply as a daughter, but as a widowed daughter, and this defined a relationship that was like a path strewn with the tiny thorns of foreboding. So how could a complete stranger like Jagmohan rend the veil of such judgements and accept her totally?

He engaged an elderly maidservant and did everything to make Nonibala feel at home. Noni had been very apprehensive that Jagmohan wouldn't accept food from her hands – she was a fallen woman, after all. As things turned out, Jagmohan was unwilling to accept food except from her hands; he even swore that unless she cooked his meals and served them herself, he wouldn't eat at all.

Jagmohan knew another round of condemnation was imminent. Noni too knew this and had no end of anxiety on this account. It started in a few days. The maidservant had taken Noni to be Jagmohan's daughter. Then one day she came and after heaping abuse on Noni walked out on her job with a display of great disgust. Noni grew despondent out of solicitude for Jagmohan. He comforted her, saying, '*Ma*, the full moon has risen in my house, so it's time for the flood-tide of calumny to rise. But however muddy the waves, they can't taint my moonlight.'

An aunt on Jagmohan's father's side walked over from Harimohan's part of the house and said, 'How disgusting, Jagai! Get rid of this sin.'

'You people are religious,' Jagmohan said, 'so you can say such a thing. But if I get rid of the sin, what is to be the fate of the poor sinner?'

A distant cousin of his grandmother came and advised, 'Send the girl to hospital. Harimohan is willing to bear all expenses.'

'But she is a mother,' Jagmohan replied. 'Can I send a mother to hospital for no reason, just because money is available for the purpose? What sort of logic does Harimohan follow?'

'Who do you call a mother?', said the cousin, raising her eyebrows.

'A person who nurtures life in her womb, who risks her own life to give birth to her child. The heartless creature who fathered the child I'll never call a father. That fellow only puts the girl in trouble but doesn't face any trouble himself.'

Harimohan was overcome with disgust, as if his entire body had been soaked in filth. How could one bear the thought that on the other side of the boundary wall of a respectable home, on property that had come down from one's revered ancestors, a fallen woman lived so brazenly?

Harimohan readily believed that Sachish was intimately involved in this heinous sin and was indulged in it by his atheist uncle. Wherever he went he spread this tale with great outrage.

Jagmohan didn't do anything to stem the tide of obloquy.

'The religious scriptures of us atheists decree the hellfire of calumny as the prize for good deeds,' he pronounced.

The more varied and colourful the rumours that spread, the more Jagmohan and Sachish gave themselves up to satiric merriment. To joke with one's nephew over something so sordid was unheard-of by Harimohan or respectable citizens like him.

Purandar hadn't stepped into Jagmohan's part of the house since it was partitioned. But he now swore that his prime task in life was to drive the girl out of the neighbourhood.

Jagmohan, when he went to school, secured all entrances to his house and, whenever during the day he could take some time off, didn't fail to come and check if everything was safe.

One day around noon Purandar placed a ladder against the parapet of the roof on his father's half of the house and descended into Jagmohan's portion. Nonibala had finished her midday meal and dozed off, leaving the door of her room open.

Purandar entered the room and, seeing her, roared in anger and surprise, 'So! You are here!'

Startled out of sleep, Noni's face turned pale at the sight of Purandar. She didn't have the strength to flee or to say anything. Quivering with rage, Purandar called her name, 'Noni!'

Just at that moment Jagmohan entered the room from behind and screamed, 'Get out! Get out of my house!'

Purandar puffed up like an enraged cat.

'If you don't leave at once I'll call the police,' Jagmohan threatened.

Purandar shot a fiery glance at Noni and left. Noni fainted.

Jagmohan understood now. When he asked Sachish he found that Sachish knew it was Purandar who had ruined the girl's life, but had kept the information from Jagmohan lest he became angry and created an uproar. Sachish knew that Noni wouldn't be safe from Purandar's persecution anywhere else in Calcutta; if there was any place where Purandar wouldn't dare intrude it was his uncle's house.

Seized with fear, Noni trembled like a bamboo shoot for several days, then gave birth to a stillborn child.

Purandar had literally kicked Noni out one midnight, and had then, for a long time, looked for her in vain. On discovering her in his uncle's house he burned from top to toe with jealousy. He assumed that Sachish had enticed her away to keep her for his own enjoyment and had put her up in Jagmohan's house in order to add insult to injury. On no account could this be tolerated.

Harimohan came to know of all this. In fact Purandar felt no embarrassment about letting his father find out. Harimohan looked upon his son's misdeeds with something like affectionate indulgence. He considered it highly unnatural and immoral of Sachish to snatch the girl from Purandar. It became his firm resolve that Purandar should avenge the insufferable insult and injustice by retrieving what was rightfully his. He put up money to hire the services of a woman who would pose as Noni's mother and plead with Jagmohan to give back her daughter. But Jagmohan drove the imposter away with such a terrible look on his face that she didn't dare go back.

Noni grew emaciated day by day, till she seemed about to fade away into her shadow. The Christmas holiday had come; Jagmohan didn't leave her alone in the house even for a moment.

One evening he was reading a novel by Scott and retelling the story to Noni in Bengali. Just then Purandar stormed into the room with another youth. When Jagmohan rose with threats to call the police, the youth insisted, 'I am Noni's brother, I have come to take her home.'

Without another word Jagmohan grabbed Purandar by the neck, marched him to the stairs and with one shove sent him clattering on his way. To the youth he thundered, 'Have you no shame? When Noni needs protection you are nowhere around, and when people try to ruin her you join them saying you are her brother!'

The young man backed away quickly, but from a distance he shouted back that he would seek police assistance to rescue his sister. He was indeed Noni's brother; Purandar had asked him along in order to make out that it was Sachish who had brought about Noni's ruin.

Noni prayed silently, 'O Mother Earth, swallow me up.'

Jagmohan called Sachish and said, 'Let me take Noni to some town upcountry. I'll find some sort of a job. The persecution has reached such a pitch that the poor girl won't survive here much longer.'

'When my elder brother is involved the persecution will follow wherever you go,' Sachish replied.

'Then what is to be done?'

'There is a way out. I'll marry Noni.'

'Marry?'

'Yes, according to Civil Law.'

Jagmohan hugged Sachish to his chest. Tears streamed from his eyes. He had never shed such tears at his age.

6

Since the partition of the house Harimohan hadn't visited Jagmohan even once. One day he turned up suddenly, all dishevelled and distraught. '*Dada*,' he said, 'what's this disaster I've been hearing about?'

'Disaster was imminent, but a way has been found to avert it.'

'*Dada*, Sachish is like a son to you – how can you let him marry that fallen woman?'

'I have brought up Sachish like a son, and my efforts have borne fruit today. He has done something to gladden our hearts.'

'*Dada*, I'll surrender to you – I'll give up half my income to you – please don't wreak such terrible vengeance on me.'

Jagmohan stood up from the cot on which he was sitting.

'Indeed! You have come to pacify the dog with the leavings on your plate! I'm not a pious man like you, I'm an atheist, remember that. I don't seek revenge in anger, nor do I accept charity.'

Next, Harimohan turned up at Sachish's lodgings. He drew him aside and said, 'What's that I hear? Couldn't you find some other way to ruin your life? How can you dishonour the family like this?'

'I wasn't keen on marriage,' Sachish replied, 'but I'm trying to erase the stain of dishonour from our family.'

'Haven't you any moral sense?' Harimohan said. 'That girl is virtually your *Dada*'s wife, yet you . . .'

'Virtually his wife?' Sachish interrupted in protest. 'Don't you dare say such a thing.'

After that Harimohan hurled at Sachish whatever abuse came to his mind. Sachish made no reply.

Harimohan found himself in dire straits because Purandar was shamelessly telling everybody that he would commit suicide if Sachish married Noni. 'That would end the bother,' Purandar's wife said, 'but you don't have the guts to do it.' Harimohan didn't quite believe Purandar's threat, but neither could he stop worrying about it.

Sachish had avoided Noni's company all these days. He hadn't ever seen her alone, and it was doubtful if he had exchanged even a couple of words with her. When the final arrangements for the marriage had been made Jagmohan told Sachish, 'Before the wedding you ought to have a word with Noni in private. You need to know each other's true feelings.'

Sachish agreed.

Jagmohan set a date. '*Ma*,' he said to Noni when the day arrived. 'You must dress up now to my liking.'

Noni lowered her eyes bashfully.

'No, *Ma*, don't be shy. It's my fond wish to see you fully decked out today. Please satisfy my whim.'

He then handed her a set of clothes he had bought himself – a gilt-embroidered Benares sari, blouse and veil.

Noni reverently bent down to take the dust of his feet. He hastily drew back his feet and said, 'In all these days I've failed to rid you of your reverence for me. I may be older in years, but you, *Ma*, are greater than I because you are a mother.'

Then kissing the top of her head he said, 'I have an invitation to Bhabatosh's – I may be a little late.'

Noni took his hand. '*Baba*,' she said, 'give me your blessing today.'

'*Ma*, I can see very clearly that you'll turn this old atheist, in his dotage, into a believer. I don't care a straw about blessings, but when I see that face of yours I must confess I do feel like blessing you.'

He took her chin to raise her face and gazed silently at it; tears streamed from her eyes.

That evening messengers hastened to Bhabatosh's to call Jagmohan home. When he came he saw Noni lying in bed in the clothes he had given her, clutching a note in her hand. Sachish was at the head of the bed. Jagmohan opened the note and read:

> *Baba*, I can't go on. Please forgive me. All these days I have tried heart and soul for your sake, but I can't even now forget him. A million obeisances on your blessed feet.
>
> The sinner Nonibala

Sachish

On his deathbed Jagmohan said to Sachish, 'If you fancy a *sraddha* have one for your father, but not for your uncle.'

This is how he died. When the plague first came to Calcutta people were more fearful of the uniformed government employees who carted victims off to quarantine than of the disease itself. Harimohan reckoned that the tanners in the neighbourhood would be among the first to catch the disease; and then his family would surely die with those wretches. Before escaping to safety, he approached his brother with an offer. '*Dada*,' he said, 'I've found a house in Kalna, on the bank of Ganges. If you . . .'

'Splendid!' Jagmohan said. 'But how can I abandon these people?'

'Who?'

'The tanners.'

Harimohan made a wry face and left. He went to Sachish's lodgings and said, 'Come with us.'

'I have work to do,' Sachish said.

'What, playing undertaker to those tanners?'

'Well, yes, if necessary.'

'Necessary indeed! It seems you might consider it necessary to consign your ancestors to hell, you wicked atheist.'

Harimohan saw ominous signs of apocalypse, and returned home filled with despair. That day, to bring himself luck, he filled a quire of paper with the holy name of Durga in a minuscule hand.

Harimohan left Calcutta. The plague reached the neighbourhood. Victims were reluctant to call in a doctor lest he force them to move into hospital. Jagmohan visited the plague hospitals.

Saying on his return, 'Should the sick be treated like criminals?' he converted his house into a hospital. Sachish and a handful of us were volunteer nurses; a doctor also joined our team.

Our first patient was a Muslim; he died. The second was Jagmohan himself; he didn't survive either. 'The creed I have lived by all my life has given me its parting gift,' he said to Sachish. 'I have no regrets.'

Sachish, who had never made obeisance to Uncle when he was alive, bent down and for the first and last time reverently touched his feet.

When Harimohan next met Sachish he said, 'This is how atheists meet their end.'

'Exactly!' said Sachish with pride.

2

Just as the light of a lamp put out by a puff of breath vanishes instantly, after Jagmohan's death Sachish disappeared – we didn't know where.

It's impossible for us to imagine how much Sachish loved Uncle. Uncle was Sachish's father, friend, and even – in a sense – his son. For he was so absent-minded about himself and so ignorant of wordly affairs, that one of Sachish's prime responsibilities was to keep him out of trouble. Thus it was through Uncle that Sachish acquired what was his own and gave away what he had to contribute of his own.

It is also futile to try to imagine how Sachish was affected by the void left by Uncle's death. Sachish struggled in intolerable anguish to establish that the void could never in fact be so empty, that no emptiness was so absolute that it left no room for truth. For if it wasn't the case that what was 'No' in one sense was also 'Yes' in another, then through the tiny hole of that 'No' the entire universe would vanish into nothingness.

Sachish roamed the countryside for two years, and I had no contact with him. Our group continued with its activities with increased vigour. We became the scourge of those who had any kind of religious belief, and deliberately undertook charitable work of the sort that would not win the approval of our more respectable contemporaries. Sachish had been the flower in our midst; when he stepped aside only our naked thorns were displayed.

3

We had no news of Sachish for two years. I don't wish to say anything critical about Sachish but I couldn't help thinking then that at the shock of bereavement the note to which he had been tuned had slid down the scale.

'Just as a moneychanger rings a coin to test if it is counterfeit,' Uncle had once remarked on seeing a *sannyasi*, 'the world tests the quality of man by making him experience loss, bereavement and the lure of salvation. Coins that ring false are discarded as counterfeit; these *sannyasis* are like those fake coins, useless in life's transactions. Yet they go around saying that they have renounced the world. If one is of any use there's no way one can slip out of the world of *samsara*. Dry leaves fall from the boughs because the tree shakes them off – they are trash after all.'

Among so many was it going to be Sachish's lot to end up as trash? Had it been inscribed on the dark touchstone of grief that Sachish was worthless in life's marketplace?

Then we heard that Sachish was somewhere in Chittagong. *Our* Sachish was with Swami Lilananda, dancing ecstatically, singing *kirtans*, playing cymbals, and rousing whole neighbourhoods into a state of excitement.

Once I couldn't imagine how someone like Sachish could be an atheist; now I couldn't understand how Swami Lilananda made Sachish dance to his tune.

Meanwhile how could we not lose face? Our enemies would laugh at us. And they were far from few.

Members of our group turned violently against Sachish. Many claimed to have known all along that there was no real substance to Sachish; he was all empty theory.

I realized now how much I loved Sachish. He had aimed a fatal missile at our group, yet I couldn't bring myself to feel any anger towards him.

4

I set out in search of Swami Lilananda. I had to cross many rivers, cut across many fields, spend nights in grocers' stalls, before finally catching up with Sachish in a village. It was about two in the afternoon.

I wanted to see him alone, but there was no hope of that. The courtyard of the disciple's house in which the Swami had halted was thick with people. There had been *kirtan* singing all morning. Arrangements were afoot to provide a meal to those who had come from afar.

As soon as he saw me Sachish rushed forward and hugged me. I was astonished. Sachish had always been restrained in manner; with him, silence evinced depth of feeling. Today he seemed as if high on drugs.

The Swami was resting in a room. The door was slightly ajar. He caught sight of me and called out in a deep voice, 'Who is it?'

'My friend Sribilash,' said Sachish.

My name had begun to get around. A certain Englishman of intellectual repute had observed on hearing me lecture in English, 'The fellow's quite . . .' but let me not make more enemies by going into all that. I had become well known among students and their parents as a formidable atheist who could drive the four-horse carriage of English conversation at twenty or twenty-five miles an hour with amazing finesse.

I believe the Swami was pleased to hear of my arrival. He wished to see me. I entered his room and greeted him with a *namaskar*. It was a *namaskar* in which my joined palms rose perpendicularly to my forehead; my head didn't bow at all. We were Uncle's disciples, our *namaskar* was like an unstrung bow: dispensing with the *nama*, it stood ramrod straight.

Noticing this, the Swami said, 'Get the hookah ready for me, Sachish.'

Sachish sat down to prepare the hookah. As the *tikka* lit up I too began to burn. I couldn't decide where to sit. The only furniture was the cot on which the Swami had made his bed. I didn't consider it improper to sit down on one side of it, but I didn't do so, I don't know why – I kept standing by the door.

I discovered that the Swamiji knew I had won the Premchand-Raychand scholarship. '*Baba*,' he said, 'the diver has to go down to the seabed to look for pearls, but it's fatal to get stuck there, so he comes gasping to the surface to save his life. If you want salvation you must leave the floor of the ocean of knowledge and come to the shore. You have won the Premchand-Raychand scholarship, now look to the Premchand-Raychand renunciationship!'

When the hookah was ready Sachish handed it to him and sat on the floor at his feet. The Swami at once stretched out his legs towards Sachish, who began slowly massaging them.

The sight was so distressing to me that I couldn't remain any longer in the room. I realized it was in order to provoke me that Sachish had been made to prepare the Swami's hookah and massage his legs.

The Swami continued with his rest, the visitors finished their meal of *khichuri*. At five, *kirtan* singing resumed and went on till ten at night.

Catching Sachish alone at night I said, 'Sachish, from the moment you were born you have lived in a liberated atmosphere. What strange bondage have you got yourself into now? Can Uncle's death be such a devastating event?'

Partly as an affectionate joke, partly because of my appearance, Sachish used to transpose the first two syllables of my name, Sribilash, and call me Bisri, which means ugly. 'Bisri,' he said, 'when Uncle was alive he gave me freedom in the sphere of life's activities, and this was like the freedom a child enjoys in the playpen. With his death he has set me free in the ocean of ecstasy, which offers the freedom a child finds at its mother's breast. Having enjoyed the freedom of daylight, why should I now forgo the freedom of the night world? You may rest assured Uncle has had a hand in both.'

'Whatever you say,' I retorted, 'Uncle's weaknesses didn't extend to making others massage his legs and prepare his hookah. This doesn't look like liberation.'

'Uncle trained my limbs for work and gave me the freedom of

the shore,' said Sachish. 'Now I am in the ocean of ecstasy, where a boat's moorings are its guarantee of liberty. That is why the guru has bound me like this to a life of service; by massaging his legs I am making my way across the ocean.'

'The words don't sound unattractive on your lips,' I said, 'but the person who stretches out his legs towards you like that is surely . . .'

'He can do that because he doesn't really need anyone's service. If he did he would feel embarrassed; the need is mine alone.'

I realized that Sachish was in a realm I had never entered. The 'me' whom Sachish had embraced when we met wasn't 'me, Sribilash', it was the Universal Soul that inheres in all beings, it was an Idea.

Such an Idea is like wine; whoever is drunk with it will clasp anyone to his breast and shed tears; it makes no difference whether that one is me or another. But I couldn't share the inebriate's joy; I didn't want to lose my power of discrimination and be a mere ripple in a flood of Sameness – after all, 'I' am 'me'.

I knew it wasn't a question that could be settled through argument. But it was beyond me to abandon Sachish; drawn into the Swami's group because of him, I too drifted from village to village. Gradually the intoxication came to possess me as well; I too embraced everyone, shed unrestrained tears, massaged the guru's legs; and one day in a sudden, ineffable rapture I saw Sachish assume an other-worldly form that could only be that of a god.

5

Having roped two formidable English-educated atheists into his fold, Swami Lilananda's fame spread far and wide. His disciples in Calcutta implored him to make his base in the city. So he went.

The Swami once had an extremely devoted disciple named Shibtosh, with whom he would stay whenever he was in Calcutta. The pride and joy of Shibtosh's life was to serve the Swami and his retinue.

Before his death Shibtosh made out a will granting liferent for his house and other property in Calcutta to his young and childless wife, and ultimate ownership to his guru; it was his wish that in time the house would become the chief place of pilgrimage for his guru's followers. This was where we billeted.

During my delirious wanderings from village to village, I had been in one frame of mind. After coming to Calcutta I found it difficult to sustain my drunkenness. All these days I had been in the realm of ecstasy, where the Cosmic Female and the consciousness pervading Male made love endlessly; the music of that cosmic romance filled the village pastures, the peepul-shade at the river-crossing, leisurely afternoons, and the evening pulsating with the chirp of crickets. It was like a dream in which I floated without hindrance in the open sky; coming to the tough city my head suffered a knock, I was jostled by crowds – the spell broke. Once in lodgings in this very Calcutta I had devoted myself day and night to study; had met with friends by the Goldighi lake to ponder the nation's future; played the volunteer at political conferences; nearly landed in jail in protesting against police brutality. Responding to Uncle's call, I had vowed to oppose the brigandage of society with my last breath and to liberate the minds of my countrymen from all forms of bondage. From early youth till now I had moved through the city throngs like a sailboat travelling proudly upstream with chest puffed out, derided by stranger and kinsman alike. Now in this same Calcutta, I tried desperately to sustain the trance of lachrymose ecstasy amidst crowds tossed about by hunger and thirst, pleasure and pain, and the baffling problems of good and evil. At times I felt I was too weak, I was straying, my devotions lacked concentration. But turning to Sachish I saw in his face no recognition of the fact that Calcutta had a position in geographical space; to him it was all shadow.

6

My friend and I continued to live with our guru in Shibtosh's house. We were his chief disciples and he wanted us to be constantly with him.

Day and night we discoursed with our guru and fellow disciples on the theory of *rasa*, the essence of ecstasy. Amidst the obscure profundities loud feminine laughter would suddenly reach us from the zenana. Sometimes we would hear a loud summons to the maid, 'Bami!' Seen from the rare heights of abstraction in which our minds were absorbed these were trivialities; but it would suddenly seem as if a shower had pattered down in the middle of a drought. Whenever such small signs of life in the hidden world on the other side of the wall touched us like falling petals, I would be struck by the realization that the desired partner in ecstasy was there – where the rattling bunch of household keys was tied to a corner of Bami's sari, where the smell of cooking rose from the kitchen, where I could hear the sound of sweeping, where all was trivial yet true, where the sweet and the bitter, the crude and the subtle, were inextricably intertwined – there lay the paradise of ecstasy.

The widow's name was Damini. At first we would catch only fleeting glimpses of her, but Sachish and I were so close to the guru that she couldn't keep herself hidden from us for long.

Damini means lightning and Damini was like the lightning in thunderous monsoon clouds. Her outward form brimmed with youthful vitality; and in her soul danced a restless flame.

At one point in his diary Sachish noted:

'In Nonibala I saw one form of the Universal Feminine – the woman who takes upon herself the stigma of sin, who sacrifices her life for a sinner's sake, who in dying adds to the contents of life's cup of ambrosia. In Damini the Universal Feminine assumes another form. She has no truck with death, she is a celebrant of the vital force. Like a spring garden she is always brimming with waves of lovely fragrance. She doesn't want to renounce anything in life; she is unwilling to play host to the *sannyasi*; she has sworn not to pay a paisa in homage to the cold north wind.'

Let me say a few words about Damini's background. Damini's marriage took place at a time when her father Annadaprasad's coffers overflowed with a sudden flood of profit from the jute trade. Till then Shibtosh had only a good pedigree; now fortune smiled on him. Annadaprasad presented his son-in-law with a house in Calcutta and arranged for him an income sufficient to ensure a comfortable life. The dowry also included a large quantity of ornaments.

He tried to train up Shibtosh in his office. But it wasn't in Shibtosh's nature to take an interest in worldly matters. An astrologer once told him that the influence of Jupiter during a certain conjunction would liberate him from earthly attachments. Henceforth, in anticipation of his salvation, he decided to forgo the desire for gold and other precious substances. He had by then become a disciple of Swami Lilananda.

Meanwhile a crosswind in business had overturned the full-sailed pinnace of Annadaprasad's fortune. He had to sell off everything, even his house, and was hard put to provide his family with regular meals.

One evening Shibtosh entered the zenana and told his wife, 'Swamiji is here – he has asked to see you to give some advice.'

'I can't go now. I don't have any time,' Damini said.

No time! Shibtosh drew closer and saw that in the darkened room Damini had taken her jewellery out of its boxes.

'What are you doing?' he asked.

'I am sorting out my jewellery,' Damini replied.

Was that why she had no time? Really! The next day Damini opened the steel chest and found her jewellery gone.

'Where's my jewellery?' she demanded of her husband.

'You have presented it to your guru,' her husband said. 'That was why he had summoned you at that moment, for he is omniscient. He has liberated you now from desire for gold.'

Damini flared up. 'Give me back my jewellery!'

'Why, what for?' her husband asked.

'It was my father's gift,' Damini replied. 'I'll return it to him.'

'It has fallen into better hands,' said Shibtosh. 'Instead of going to feed those with earthly attachments it has been dedicated to the service of religious devotees.'

Thus began the brigandage in the name of spiritual devotion. In order to rid Damini of the spirits of all earthly desires, the exorcist's raids continued apace. While Damini's father and young brothers starved, she cooked daily, with her own hands, for sixty to seventy devotees. She would wilfully put no salt in the curry, she would let the milk go off: such was her brand of asceticism.

Just then her husband died after imposing on her a penalty for her lack of devotion. Together with all his property he placed his wife under the guardianship of the guru.

7

Throughout the house the tide of devotion rose tirelessly. People thronged from far away to seek the guru's blessing. Yet Damini, who could come close to him without trying, kept this precious opportunity at bay with continuous taunts and insults.

Whenever the guru asked to see her to impart some special advice she would say, 'I have a headache.' If he questioned her about a slip-up in the dinner arrangements she would say, 'I was out at the theatre.' It wasn't true, but it was barbed. The guru's women devotees saw how she behaved and raised their eyebrows in disbelief. To begin with, Damini didn't dress like a widow; then, she would pointedly ignore the guru's instructions; and finally she showed no hint of the radiance of ascetic purity that lights up body and soul through being close to such a great man. Everybody voiced the same opinion: 'Some creature indeed! We have seen a lot, but such a woman – never!'

The Swamiji would laugh and say, 'The Lord loves to wrestle with a strong opponent. When she eventually concedes defeat, she will be struck dumb for ever.'

He began showing excessive forgiveness towards her. This was even more intolerable to Damini, for it was merely a disguised form of punishment. One day when Damini was with a female friend he overheard her mimicking, amidst merry laughter, the exceedingly lenient manner he adopted with her.

He said nonetheless, 'God is using Damini as an agent for bringing about the unexpected. She isn't to blame.'

So far we had seen one side of Damini; now the unexpected did indeed begin.

I don't feel like writing any more; it's also hard to put these things into words. In life the web of suffering that is spun by invisible hands working behind the scene has a pattern that is neither dictated by scripture nor made to anybody's order; that's why inner and outer awkwardness forces us to suffer so many knocks, why life explodes with such sobs.

The brittle armour of rebellion silently shattered and fell off in the light of an unforeseen dawn, and the blossom of self-sacrifice raised its dew-laden head. Damini's service now became so effortlessly splendid that it seemed to spread a rare boon of sweetness over the devotions of the disciples.

When Damini's thunder and lightning had thus mellowed into a steady glow, Sachish began to notice her loveliness. But in my opinion Sachish saw only Damini's beauty, he didn't see Damini herself.

In Sachish's sitting room a photograph of Swami Lilananda in meditation had been placed on a slab of china. One day he found it in splinters on the floor. Sachish thought it was his pet cat's doing. From time to time many such accidents occurred that would be beyond the strength of a wild cat to bring about.

The atmosphere around us became charged with restless energy. Invisible lightning flickered in hidden recesses. I don't know about the others, but my soul throbbed with pain. At times I thought I wouldn't be able to bear the ceaseless play of the waves of ecstasy any longer; I felt like escaping it at a gallop. Those bygone discussions with tanners' children on Bengali conjunct letters, so utterly devoid of ecstasy as they were, seemed preferable.

One winter afternoon, the disciples were tired and the guru was resting in his room. Sachish, who needed to go there for something or the other, stopped short in the doorway. He saw Damini prostrate, with hair let down, repeatedly banging her forehead on the floor and muttering, 'O stone, stone, have mercy, have mercy on me, strike me dead!'

Sachish shivered all over with fright; he withdrew as fast as he could.

8

Once a year, in the winter month of Magh, Guruji went away to some remote, solitary place. The time had come round again.

'I'll go with you,' Sachish said.

'Me too,' I said. The pursuit of ecstasy had left me with frayed nerves. I badly needed a spell of fatiguing travel and solitary living.

Swamiji called Damini and said, '*Ma*, I'm setting off on my travels. As in the past I will arrange to send you to your aunt for the duration of the trip.'

'I will go with you,' she replied.

'How can you?' Swamiji said. 'It'll be a hard journey.'

'I'll manage,' Damini said. 'You won't have to worry about me.'

The Swami was pleased at Damini's new devotion. In past years this had been the time for Damini's holiday; she would yearn for it all year long. 'What a miracle!' mused the Swami. 'How the divine chemistry of ecstasy softens even stone.'

Damini wasn't to be put off; she came along.

9

After walking six hours in the sun that day we reached a promontory jutting into the sea. It was absolutely quiet and deserted; the susurrus of leaves in a coconut grove mingled with the lazy rumble of a nearly still sea.

It seemed to me as if a slumbering earth had stretched a weary arm over the sea. In the hand at the end of that arm stood a blue-green hill. There were ancient rock carvings in a cave in the side of that hill. Whether these were Hindu or Buddhist, whether the figures were of Buddha or Krishna, whether their craftsmanship betrayed Greek influence, these were contentious issues among scholars.

We were supposed to return to human habitation after seeing the cave. But that proved impossible. The sun had nearly set and it was the twelfth day of the dark half of the lunar month.

'We shall have to spend the night in the cave,' Guruji said.

We went and sat on the sandy beach between the sea and the edge of the grove. The sun was on the sea's western rim: the departing day's final bow before the advancing dark. Guruji struck up a song – a modern poet's lyrics, which he sang in his own style:

> 'Travelling, we meet
> at day's end.
> The evening glow
> vanishes when we go
> towards it.'

That day the magic in the song was realized. Tears rolled out of Damini's eyes. Swamiji took up the middle stanza:

> 'Whether or not we meet
> I shall not grieve,
> Just pause a moment
> While I cover your feet
> in my loosened hair.'

When the Swami ended the song, the silence of the evening, filling sky and sea, swelled from the lingering essence of the tune into a ripe golden fruit. Damini prostrated herself in a *pranam* before the Swami. For a long while she didn't raise her head; her loosened hair lay piled on the sand.

10

An extract from Sachish's diary:

'The cave had many chambers. I spread my blanket in one and lay down.

'The darkness of the cave was like a black beast – its moist breath seemed to touch my skin. It seemed to me like the first animal to appear in the very first cycle of creation; it had no eyes, no ears, only a huge appetite. It had been trapped for eternity in that cave. It didn't have a mind; it knew nothing but felt pain – it sobbed noiselessly.

'Weariness like a heavy weight bore down on my entire body, yet I couldn't sleep. A bird, perhaps a bat, either came in or went out, travelling from darkness to darkness with a flailing noise from its wings. I broke into gooseflesh at the touch of the air stirred by it.

'I thought I would sleep outside the cave. But I had forgotten the way to the entrance. When I crawled forward, in one direction my head touched the ceiling; in another direction I bumped my head; in yet another I slipped into a small ditch filled with water that had seeped through a crack.

'Finally I gave up and lay down on the blanket. It seemed the primordial beast had thrust me deep into its saliva-drenched maw; there was no escape. The beast was all dark hunger, it would lick at me slowly and consume me. Its saliva was acidic, it would corrode me.

'If only I could sleep; my wakeful mind couldn't bear the close embrace of such colossal, destructive darkness: that was possible for death alone.

'After I don't know how long, a thin sheet of numbness spread over my consciousness. At some point in that semi-conscious state I felt the touch of a deep breath close to my feet. That primordial beast!

'Then something clasped my feet. At first I thought it was a wild animal. But a wild animal is hairy, this creature wasn't. My entire body shrank at the touch. It seemed to be an unknown snake-like creature. I knew nothing of its anatomy – what its head looked like, or its trunk, or its tail – nor could I imagine how it devoured its victims. It was repulsive because of its very softness, its ravenous mass.

'I was speechless with fear and loathing. I began pushing the creature away with both feet. It seemed to place its face on my feet – it was breathing heavily – I didn't know what sort of a face it was. I began to kick at it.

'Eventually I came out of my trance. At first I had thought the creature was hairless; but suddenly I felt a mass of hair, as from a mane, fall on my feet.

'I got up quickly and sat down.

'Somebody seemed to move away in the dark. A strange sound reached my ears: such stifled sobs!'

Damini

We returned from the cave. Accommodation had been arranged for us on the upper floor of the house of one of Guruji's disciples, close by the village temple.

We didn't see much of Damini now. She cooked and served our meals but avoided our company as far as possible. She made friends with the village women and spent her time visiting their homes.

This annoyed Guruji somewhat. He felt that worldly life still attracted her more than the celestial realm. She seemed to tire of the nearly religious devotion with which she had been looking after us for some days past. She made mistakes, the natural grace with which she did things wasn't there any longer.

Guruji began to be secretly fearful of Damini once again. Her brows had for some days been darkened by a frown and her temper had become rather unpredictable. Signs of rebellion were noticeable in her lips, the corners of her eyes, the clumsily knotted hair on her neck, and at times in the involuntary motions of her hands.

Guruji once more concentrated on the devotional hymns. He thought their sweetness would draw the errant bee back to the honeycomb. The short winter days frothed and overflowed with the intoxicating brew of music.

But there was no catching Damini. 'God is out hunting,' Guruji observed with a chuckle one day, 'and the doe by leading him a chase is adding zest to the hunt; but die she must.'

When we first got acquainted with Damini she didn't appear among the disciples, but we didn't notice that. Now her absence from our midst became all too conspicuous. Not being able to see her affected us like being blown about by gusts of wind. Since Guruji interpreted her absence as pride, it hurt his pride. As for me, it's hardly necessary to talk about my feelings.

One day Guruji mustered enough resolve to put a mild request to her: 'Damini, if you can make time this afternoon . . .'

'I can't,' she said.

'Why not?'

'I've got to go to the village to help make sweets.'

'Sweets? Why?'

'There's a wedding at the Nandys'.'

'Is it absolutely essential?'

'Yes, I've promised.'

Without another word Damini left like a sudden gust of wind. Sachish was sitting with us; he was astounded. So many eminent, learned, wealthy and wise men had come with bowed heads to his guru; yet where did this slip of a girl acquire such brazen arrogance?

On another day in the evening, when Damini was home, Guruji began a ponderous sermon, speaking especially carefully. After a while he became aware of a certain blankness in our faces. He noticed that we had become inattentive. Turning round he saw that Damini was no longer where she had sat sewing buttons on shirts. He realized that both Sachish and I were filled with the same thought – that Damini had got up and left. The thought that Damini hadn't listened to him, hadn't in fact wanted to listen to his words, rattled in his mind like a tambourine. He lost the thread of his discourse. He couldn't restrain himself any longer but got up and called from outside Damini's room, 'Damini, what are you doing all by yourself? Won't you join us in the other room?'

'No, I'm busy,' Damini replied.

The Guru peeped in and saw a kite inside a cage. A couple of days back the kite had flown into a telegraph wire and fallen to the ground, where it had been set upon by crows. Damini had rescued it – and nursed it ever since.

So much for the kite. Damini had also got hold of a puppy whose appearance and pedigree matched each other perfectly. It was discord personified. At the first sound of our cymbals it raised its muzzle towards heaven and vociferously complained to God. It was a small consolation that God didn't heed the plaint, but those of us who had to hear it on earth were driven to distraction.

One day when Damini was tending some flowering plants grown on the roof in a broken pot Sachish went up to her and asked, 'Why have you stopped attending?'

'Attending what?'

'Guruji's meetings.'

'Why, what use have you people for me?'

'None, but you have some use for us.'

Damini flared up: 'Not at all!'

Sachish stared dumbfounded at her. 'Can't you see,' he said after a while, 'how uneasy you've become? If you want peace . . .'

'*You* give me peace? You've driven yourselves crazy, forever stirring up waves in your minds. Is that peace? I beg you, help me. I used to be at peace, let me live in peace again.'

'You may see waves on the surface,' Sachish said, 'but if you have the patience to dive beneath and look you'll see that all is calm.'

Joining her palms in entreaty Damini said, 'For God's sake don't ask me to dive any more. I'd feel relieved if you gave me up.'

2

I didn't have enough experience to know the secrets of the female heart. My superficial observations led me to believe that women are ready to lose their hearts where they are sure to be requited with sorrow. They will string their garland for a brute who will trample it into the horrid slime of lust; or else they will aim it at a man whose head it won't reach because he is so absorbed in a world of abstraction that he has virtually ceased to exist. When they have a chance to choose their mates women shun average men like us, who are a mixture of the crude and the refined, know Woman as women – in other words, know that women are neither clay dolls nor the vibrations of *veena* strings. Women avoid us because we offer neither the fatal attraction of murky desire nor the colourful illusion of profound abstractions; we cannot break them through the remorseless torment of lust, nor can we melt them in the heat of abstraction and recast them in the mould of our own fancy. We know them as they really are; that's why even if they like us they won't fall in love with us. We are their true refuge, they can count on our loyalty; but our self-sacrifice comes so readily they forget that it has any value. The only baksheesh we receive from them is that whenever they need us they use us, and perhaps even respect us a little, but . . . enough! These words probably stem from resentment, and probably aren't true. Perhaps it is to our advantage that we get nothing in return – at least we can console ourselves with that thought.

Damini avoided Guruji because she bore him a grudge; she avoided Sachish because she felt exactly the opposite towards him. I was the only one around for whom she felt neither anger nor attraction. For this reason whenever she got a chance Damini would chat with me about her past, her present, what she saw or heard in the neighbourhood – trivial things like that. I never imagined that such an insignificant event as Damini jabbering away as she sat slicing betel-nuts on the little veranda in front of our rooms upstairs would affect Sachish so much in his present mood of abstraction. Well, it might not have been such a trivial event, but I knew that in the realm in which Sachish existed there was no such thing as an event. The divine workings of Hladini, Sandhini and Jogmaya in that realm were a perennial romance, and therefore beyond historic time. Those who listened to the whistle of the ever-steady breeze that played there on the banks of an ever-flowing Jamuna wouldn't, surely, see or hear anything of the transitory events in the mundane world around them. At any rate, till our return from the cave Sachish's eyes and ears had been pretty inactive.

I myself was partly to blame. I had begun to play truant every now and then from our discussions on mystic ecstasy. Sachish began to notice my absence. Once he came looking for me and found me following Damini with an earthen bowl of milk that I had bought from the local cowherds to feed her pet mongoose. The task would hardly suffice as an excuse for truancy; it could have been easily postponed till the discussion ended; and in fact if the mongoose had been left to forage for its meals the principle of kindness to all creatures wouldn't have been grossly violated and my reputation for decorum would have remained intact. Consequently, I was quite flustered at Sachish's sudden appearance. I set the bowl down at once and tried to retrieve my self-esteem by sneaking away.

But Damini's behaviour was astonishing. She wasn't embarrassed at all, and asked me, 'Where are you going, Sribilashbabu?'

I scratched my head and mumbled, 'Well . . .'

'Guruji's meeting has ended by now,' Damini said, 'so why don't you sit down?'

My ears tingled with embarrassment at hearing such a request in Sachish's presence.

'There's a problem with the mongoose,' Damini said. 'Last night it stole a chicken from a Muslim house. It's not safe to let it loose. I have asked Sribilashbabu to buy a large basket to keep it in.'

Damini seemed rather keen to inform Sachish about Sribilashbabu's submissiveness in the matter of feeding milk to the mongoose or buying a basket for it. I was reminded of the day

Guruji had asked Sachish in my presence to prepare the hookah. It was the same thing.

Without a word Sachish walked away quickly. Glancing at Damini's face I saw her eyes cast lightning shafts after Sachish. Inwardly she smiled a cruel smile.

God knows what she made of the incident, but the practical outcome was that she began to seek me out on the flimsiest of pretexts. One day she cooked some sweet dish and insisted on serving it exclusively for me.

'But Sachish . . .'

'Asking him to eat will only annoy him.'

Sachish came round several times and saw me eating.

Among us three, mine was the most difficult position. The two main characters in the drama were thoroughly self-possessed in their performance. I was conspicuous for the sole reason that I was utterly insignificant. At times this made me angry with my lot, but neither could I help my craving for whatever little my auxiliary role brought me. Such dire straits!

3

For some days Sachish played his cymbals louder than ever as he danced in the chorus of *kirtan* singers. Then he came to me one day and said, 'We can't keep Damini among us.'

'Why?' I asked.

'We must sever all connection with Nature.'

'If that is so,' I retorted, 'we must admit there's a grave flaw in our spiritual endeavour.'

Sachish gave me an open-eyed stare.

'What you call Nature is a reality,' I said. 'You may shun it, but you can't leave it out of the human world. If you practise your austerities pretending it isn't there you will only delude yourself; and when the deceit is exposed there will be no escape route.'

'I'm not interested in logical quibbles,' Sachish replied. 'I am being practical. Clearly women are agents of Nature, whose dictates they carry out by adopting varied disguises to beguile the mind. They cannot fulfil their mistress's command till they have completely enslaved the consciousness. So to keep the consciousness clear we have to keep clear of these bawds of Nature.'

I was about to continue but Sachish stopped me: 'My dear Bisri, you can't see Nature's fatal charm because you have already succumbed to it. But the beautiful form with which it has bewitched you will disappear like a mask as soon as she has realized her purpose; when the time comes she will remove the very desire which has clouded your vision and made you see her as greater than anything else in the universe. When the trap of illusion is so clearly laid, why walk with bravado straight into it?'

'I accept all you are saying,' I replied, 'but I'd like to point out that I didn't myself lay this worldwide trap of Nature, and I know no way of evading it. Since we can't deny it, true devotion in my view ought to allow us to accept it and yet enable us to transcend it. Whatever you say, dear Sachish, we are not doing that, and so we are desperately trying to amputate one half of the truth.'

'Could you spell out a little more clearly what sort of spiritual path you wish to follow?' he asked.

'We must row the boat of life in Nature's current', I said. 'Our problem should not be to stop the current; our problem is to keep the boat from sinking and in motion. For that we need a rudder.'

'Our guru is that rudder,' Sachish retorted, 'but you can't see that because you don't accept him. Do you wish your spiritual development to follow your own whims? The result will be disaster.'

So saying, Sachish retired to the guru's room, sat down at his feet and began massaging them. That day, after preparing the guru's hookah, he raised with him his complaint against Nature.

The question couldn't be resolved over a single smoke. For days the guru pondered the problem from various angles. He had suffered much on account of Damini. Now it appeared that the presence of this one woman had created a whirlpool in the current of his disciples' devotion. But Shibtosh had bequeathed to him the guardianship of Damini together with the house and other property, making it difficult to get rid of her. The problem was compounded by the fact that the guru was afraid of Damini.

Meanwhile, though Sachish continued massaging the guru's feet and preparing his hookah with doubled, even quadrupled enthusiasm and increasing frequency, he couldn't be oblivious of the fact that Sachish's spiritual path had been well and truly obstructed by Nature.

One day a renowned group of *kirtan* singers from another part of the country were performing at the local Krishna-temple. The session seemed set to go on till late. I slipped away soon after the start, thinking my absence wouldn't be noticed amidst the crowd.

That evening Damini laid bare her soul. The things that are hard to say, that stick in the throat even if one wishes to say them, were said by her with a wonderful simplicity. As she spoke she seemed to discover many dark and unfamiliar corners of her own mind. Quite fortuitously she had found an opportunity to come face to face with herself.

We didn't notice when Sachish came up behind us and stood

listening. Tears were streaming from Damini's eyes. Not that what she said was very serious, but that day it all seemed to flow from the deep wellspring of her tears.

When Sachish turned up the *kirtan* session was clearly still a long way from the end. I could see that he had been agitated by something for some time.

Suddenly catching sight of Sachish standing in front of her, Damini hurriedly wiped her tears and made to retreat into the next room. In a quavering voice Sachish asked her to stop. 'Please, Damini, there's something I have to say to you.'

Damini sat down again slowly. I began to fidget, looking for an escape, but Sachish fixed me with such a stare that I didn't dare move.

'You don't share our purpose in following Guruji,' Sachish said.

'No,' Damini replied.

'Then why do you remain with us?'

Damini's eyes flashed. 'Why? Do you think I came willingly? You believers have kept this unbeliever in the fetters of belief. You have left me with no choice.'

'We've decided to pay for you to live with some female relative,' Sachish said.

'*You* have decided?'

'Yes.'

'*I* haven't.'

'Why, what objections do you have?'

'For some reason or the other one of you decides one thing, while for some other reason another one of you decides another thing; am I to be a pawn caught in the middle?'

Sachish stared in astonishment.

Damini went on. 'I didn't choose to come here to please you. I won't budge just because you are not pleased with me now and wish me to leave.'

As she spoke she pressed the edge of her sari to her face with both hands and burst into tears. She hurried into her room and shut the door.

Sachish didn't return to the *kirtan* session. He sat quietly on the dusty roof. That day the sound of distant sea-waves, swept by the south wind, rose towards the stars like sobs from deep within the earth's breast. I went out and aimlessly wandered the dark deserted village paths.

4

The Earth had girded up her loins to destroy the paradise of ecstasy in which Guruji had tried to keep us cloistered. All these days he had been pouring the wine of his mystic moods into the cup of metaphor for us to guzzle, but now the clash of a beautiful figure with the figures of speech threatened to tip the cup over and spill its contents on the ground. The signs of impending danger didn't escape the guru.

Sachish had become rather strange lately. He was like a kite whose string had just snapped – still airborne but at any moment liable to go into a spin and plummet to earth. He showed no neglect in the outward forms of devotion – *jap*, austerities, prayer, discussion – but looking into his eyes one knew that inwardly he was faltering.

And as for me, Damini left nothing to conjecture. The more she realized that Guruji secretly feared her and that Sachish was in secret agony, the more she dragged me around. It got to a point where she would suddenly appear near the door when, for instance, Guruji, Sachish and I were in earnest colloquy, and then vanish after calling out: 'Sribilashbabu, will you please come to me?' She couldn't be bothered to explain why she wanted Sribilashbabu. Guruji would give me a look, Sachish would give me a look, and, deliberating whether to get up or not, I would turn towards the door and suddenly get up and rush out. Even after I had gone an attempt would be made to keep the discussion going, but the effort would be out of all proportion to the things said; then the words would cease altogether. Thus everything became topsy-turvy and threatened to disintegrate; things just wouldn't hold together any more.

Sachish and I were the stalwarts of Guruji's camp – one might say we were to him what the mythic mounts, Airavata the elephant and Ucchaisraba the horse, were to the god Indra – so he couldn't just give up on us. He went to Damini and said, '*Ma*, we're going to some remote and inaccessible places now. You must turn back.'

'Where?'

'To your aunt's.'

'I can't.'

'Why?'

'First, because she is only a distant aunt, and second, because she is under no obligation to keep me in her house.'

'It won't cost her anything. We can . . .'

'Is it only a question of cost? It's not her responsibility to look after me and watch over me.'

'Must *I* take care of you for ever?'

'Is that for me to say?'

'Where will you go if I die?'

'Why should I have to think about that? I only know that I have no mother, no father, no home, no money, I have absolutely nothing, and that's why I am such a great burden. You gladly took the burden on yourself, you can't now shift it to somebody else's shoulder.'

As Damini walked away, Guruji invoked Lord Krishna with a sigh.

One day Damini commanded me to get her some good Bengali books. Needless to say, by good books she didn't mean devotional literature, and she had no qualms about ordering me about. She had come to see that the greatest favour she could show me was to make demands on me. There are some plants that thrive if their branches are kept trimmed: in my relationship with Damini I was like those plants.

The writer whose books I had to procure was thoroughly modern. In his writings the influence of Man was much stronger than that of Manu. The packet of books fell into Guruji's hands. 'What's this, Sribilash?' he said, raising his eyebrows. 'Why have you got these books?'

I remained silent.

Turning over a few pages Guruji said, 'I find no scent of piety in this.'

He didn't like the author at all.

'If you read with a little care you will smell the scent of truth,' I blurted out.

Truth to tell, rebellion had been brewing in my soul. The intoxication of mystic flights had given me a bad hangover. Pushing Man aside to deliberate day and night on his emotional essence had produced in me an aversion as strong as one can get.

Guruji gazed at my face for a while, then said, 'Very well, I'll read them attentively and see.'

Saying this he put the books under his pillow. I could tell he had no intention of returning them.

Damini in her room must have had an inkling of what had transpired. She came to the door and said to me, 'Those books I had asked you to order – haven't they arrived?'

I kept quiet.

'Those books aren't suitable for you, *Ma*,' Guruji said.

'How would you know?' she asked.

'And how would *you* know?' Guruji said with furrowed brow.

'I read them once before. I don't suppose you ever have.'

'So why do you need them again?'

'Your needs are never questioned. Am I alone to be denied any needs of my own?'

'You know very well I am a *sannyasi*.'

'And you know that I am not a *sannyasini*. I enjoy reading those books. Give them back?'

Guruji took the books from under the pillow and tossed them towards me. I handed them to Damini.

The upshot of this incident was that Damini now summoned me to read out to her the books she used to read in the solitude of her room. Our readings, followed by discussion, took place on the veranda. Sachish would frequently pass by, now in one direction, now in the other, longing to join us but unable to do so unasked.

Once as we came to an amusing episode in a book Damini burst into uncontrollable giggles. There was a fair going on at the temple and we knew Sachish had gone there. But suddenly he came out through the back door and sat down with us.

Damini's merriment ceased instantly. I too felt discomfited. I thought I should say something to Sachish, however trivial it might be, but couldn't think of anything, and silently went on turning the pages of the book. Sachish got up and left as suddenly as he had come. After that we couldn't go on with our reading that day. Sachish perhaps didn't realize that while he envied the absence of any barrier between Damini and me, I actually envied the barrier between him and Damini.

The same day Sachish went to Guruji with a request: 'Master, I wish to go alone to the seaside for a few days. I'll be back in about a week.'

'Excellent idea,' said Guruji enthusiastically. 'By all means go.'

Sachish went away. Damini stopped asking me to read; nor did she need me for anything else. I didn't even see her go to gossip with the village women. She kept to her room, her door shut tight.

A few days went by. One day when Guruji was taking a midday nap and I sat writing a letter on the upper veranda, Sachish suddenly arrived and without a glance at me knocked on Damini's door and called, 'Damini! Damini!'

Damini at once opened the door and came out. How his face had changed! It gave the impression of a storm-tossed ship with tattered sails and broken masts. A strange look in his eyes, hair awry, face haggard, clothes dirty.

'Damini,' Sachish said, 'it was wrong of me to ask you to leave. Please forgive me.'

'Why are you saying such things?' Damini asked with palms joined submissively.

'No, really, please forgive me. I'll never again entertain for a moment the utterly unjust thought that to preserve our spirituality we can decide to keep you or abandon you, as the whim takes us. But I have a request that you must keep.'

At once bowing and touching his feet Damini said, 'I am yours to command.'

'Come and join us,' Sachish said. 'Don't hold yourself aloof like this.'

'Yes, I will join you,' Damini said. 'I won't break any rules.' She bent down again, touched Sachish's feet in obeisance and repeated, 'I won't break any rules.'

5

The rock melted again. Damini's blinding radiance retained its light but lost its heat. A sweet aura pervaded her prayers and acts of kindness. She would never miss the sessions of *kirtan* singing or discussion, in which Guruji expounded the *Bhagavad Gita* or the *Puranas*. Her dress too changed; once again she wore tussore. Whenever one saw her during the day one felt that she had just had a bath.

Damini's greatest trial lay in her behaviour with Guruji. Whenever she bowed to him I would detect a flash of fierce rage in a corner of her eye. I knew that deep in her heart she couldn't abide any of Guruji's commands; but she followed all his injunctions so completely that one day he ventured to put forth his objections to the insufferable writings of that ultra-modern writer she had asked for. The next day he found some flowers beside the bed on which he took his siesta, arranged on pages torn from that fellow's books.

I had often noticed that what Damini found most intolerable was for Guruji to command Sachish to wait on him. She would try to thrust herself forward to take Sachish's task on herself, but it wasn't always possible. So, while Sachish blew on the tobacco-bowl of Guruji's hookah, Damini desperately mumbled to herself, 'I won't break the rules, I won't break the rules . . .'

But things didn't turn out the way Sachish had expected. The last time Damini had humbled herself like this Sachish had seen only the sweetness, not the bee who produced the sweetness. This time Damini herself had become so real to him that she jostled the words of hymns and the teachings of scripture and made her presence felt: there was no way she could be suppressed. Sachish became so aware of her that his mystic trance broke. He could no longer regard her as a metaphor for a transcendental mood. Damini didn't embellish the songs any more; the songs embellished her.

Here I may as well add the simple fact that Damini had no more use for me. Her demands ended suddenly. Of my few companions the kite had died, the mongoose had fled, the puppy had been given away because its unseemly behaviour annoyed Guruji. Unemployed and companionless in this way, I went back to my old place in Guruji's court, even though the songs and the conversation I heard there had become utterly distasteful to me.

6

One day while Sachish was brewing a wonderful concoction in the open cauldron of his fancy, compounded of philosophy, science, aesthetics and theology, drawn from the past and the present of both the East and the West, Damini suddenly ran towards us and called, 'Please come quickly!'

I got up hurriedly and asked, 'What's the matter?'

'I think Nabin's wife has swallowed poison,' Damini said.

Nabin was related to one of Guruji's disciples. He was a neighbour and sang *kirtans* with our group. We found when we got there that his wife had died. On enquiry we learned that Nabin's wife had brought her motherless sister to live with her. Theirs was a *kulin* Brahmin family, so it wasn't easy to find a suitable match for the girl. She was good-looking. Nabin's younger brother chose her for his bride. He was still a college student in Calcutta, and it was understood that after taking his finals, which were due in a few months, he would marry her in the month of Ashar. Just then Nabin's wife discovered that a mutual attraction had developed between her husband and her sister. She asked him to marry her sister. Not much persuasion was necessary. Now that the nuptials were over, Nabin's first wife had committed suicide by swallowing poison.

There was nothing we could do. We came back. The disciples flocking round Guruji began singing *kirtans* to him; he joined in and began to dance.

The moon had risen in the evening sky. Damini sat quietly in a corner of the roof dappled with light and shade by the overhanging branches of a *chalta* tree. Sachish slowly paced up and down the covered veranda at the back. Keeping a diary was a weakness of mine; alone in my room I scribbled away.

The cuckoo was sleepless that night. The leaves of trees glittered in the moonlight and at the touch of the southerly breeze seemed to want to burst into speech. At one point, impelled by some notion or the other, Sachish suddenly went and stood behind Damini. She was startled and, drawing the edge of her sari over her head, she rose in a hurry – but before she could leave, Sachish called her name.

She stopped short. With joined palms she beseeched, 'Listen to me a moment, Master.'

Sachish gazed at her face in silence. 'Please explain to me,' Damini said, 'what use to the world are the things that engross you so day in and day out? Who have you succeeded in saving?'

I came out of my room and stood on the veranda. Damini went on: 'Day and night you go on about ecstasy, you talk of nothing else. Today you have seen what ecstasy is, haven't you? It was no regard for morals or a code of conduct, for brother or wife or family pride. It has no mercy, no shame, no sense of propriety. What have you devised to save man from the hell of this cruel, shameless, fatal ecstasy?'

I couldn't restrain myself and blurted out, 'We have planned to drive Woman far from our sphere and then devote ourselves undisturbed to the pursuit of ecstasy.'

Without paying any heed to my words Damini said to Sachish, 'I have got nothing from your guru. He hasn't been able to calm my restless mind even for a moment. Fire cannot put out fire. The path along which your guru has been driving everyone isn't the path of non-attachment or heroism or peace. That woman who died today was killed on the path of ecstasy by the demoness of ecstasy who sucked the blood out of her heart. Haven't you seen how hideous the demoness looks? My Master, I beseech you not to sacrifice me to her. Save me! If anybody can save me it's you.'

All three of us fell silent for a while. It became so still all around that it seemed to me as if with the chirp of crickets a numbness was stealing over the pale sky.

'Tell me what I can do for you,' Sachish said.

'Be my guru,' Damini replied. 'I won't obey any other. Give me a mantra that is above all these things, something that will keep me safe. Don't even let my guardian deity come close to me.'

Standing in a daze Sachish said, 'It will be so.'

Damini made a prolonged *pranam* with her head touching Sachish's feet. She mumbled over and over, 'You are my guru, you are my guru, save me from all sin, save me, save me . . .'

POSTSCRIPT

Once more the rumour went round, and the papers reported in abusive terms that Sachish's opinions had been revised yet again. He had once loudly denied religion and caste; then one day he had just as loudly proclaimed faith in gods and goddesses, yoga and asceticism, purificatory rituals and ancestor worship and taboos – the whole lot. And yet another day he threw overboard the whole freight of beliefs and subsided into peaceful silence – what he believed and what he denied became impossible to determine. One thing was apparent: he had taken up the welfare work he had done once in the past, but the caustic combativeness was no longer in him.

The papers had many taunts and harsh words about another matter: my marriage with Damini. Not everyone will understand the mystery behind this marriage, nor is it necessary that they should.

Sribilash

An indigo factory used to stand here. It had fallen into ruins; only a few rooms still stood. Having taken a fancy to the spot I stopped here for some days on my way home after cremating Damini's remains.

The road that led from the river to the factory was lined with *sissoo* trees. The gateposts of the entrance to the indigo plantation and a bit of its boundary wall still stood, but of the plantation itself nothing was left. The only thing one could see on the plantation lands was, in one corner, the grave of a Muslim steward of the indigo factory. Lushly flowering shrubs of *akanda* and *bhantiphool* grew in the cracks in its brickwork; having tweaked the nose of death they seemed to roll with laughter in the southerly breeze, like a groom's sisters-in-law chaffing him in the bridal chamber. The banks of the plantation's large pond had collapsed and the water had dried up. On the dry bed peasants had planted a mixture of coriander and chick-peas. When I would sit of a morning on a mound of mossy bricks in the shade of a *sissoo* tree, my head would fill with the scent of coriander blossoms.

I sat and mused that the factory which today was no more than a few scattered bones in a charnel house had once brimmed with life. One might have imagined that the waves of happiness and sadness it had set off were a tempest that would never be stilled. The redoubtable sahib who on this very spot had made the blood of thousands of poor peasants run indigo blue would have seen me as just an ordinary Bengali youth. Yet the earth had quietly girdled the edge of her green sari around her waist and with a liberal plastering of clay erased all trace of him and everything of his, his factory included; whatever vestiges of the past were still visible would be totally obliterated by just one more wipe of her hand.

Such philosophizing is old hat and I haven't set out to reiterate it here. My real feeling was this: No, my dear chap, the last word isn't the daily plastering of mud, morning after morning, on the courtyard of time. The planter sahib and the terrible life of his factory have indeed been erased like a marking in the dust – but what about my Damini?

I know no one will accept what I am saying. The demystifying verses of Shankaracharya's *Mohamudgar* spare none. 'This world is illusion,' etc, etc. But Shankaracharya was a *sannyasi*. He had said such things as, 'Of what avail are wife and child?' but without grasping their significance. I am no *sannyasi*, so I know in my bones that Damini is not a dewdrop on a lotus leaf.

But I am told even some householders speak in the same world-denying terms. That may be so. They are only householders; they may lose their housewives. Their houses are *maya*, illusion; and so are their housewives. Both are man-made things, and vanish at the touch of the broom.

I haven't had time to be a householder, and – thank heaven – it's not in my temperament to be a *sannyasi*. That's why the woman I found as a companion didn't become a housewife; she couldn't be dismissed as *maya*; she was real. Till the end she remained true to her name, *Damini*, lightning. Who would dare call her a shadow?

There are many things I wouldn't have written, if I had known Damini merely as a housewife. It is because I have known her in a nobler, truer relationship that I can tell everything frankly, whatever others may say.

If I had been able to turn Damini into a regular housewife and pass my days as others do in this world of *maya*, I would have had a carefree existence, oiling my body, taking my bath, chewing *pan* after meals; and after Damini's death I would have said with a sigh, 'Varied is the world of *samsara*.' And to taste once again its variety I would have respectfully accepted the proposal of a matchmaking aunt. But a smooth entry into *samsara*, like that of feet entering an old pair of shoes, was not for me. From the start I forswore all hope of happiness. No, that's not quite true – I am human enough not to give up hope of happiness; I must have had some hope of it, but I certainly didn't feel I had a claim on it.

And why not? Because I had to persuade Damini to assent to our marriage. We didn't exchange ritual glances under the corner of a red silk shawl to the accompaniment of *Raga Shahana*. I had entered marriage in the broad light of day, with full understanding of everything involved.

When we left Swami Lilananda we were faced with the necessity of thinking about food and shelter. Till then, wherever we went we gorged on the food-offerings brought to our guru: indigestion was a greater worry than hunger. We had totally forgotten that people in this world had to build houses and maintain them, or at least rent them. All we knew was that people had to sleep in houses. As for our householder host, where he would find some space for himself wasn't our concern; but he had to worry all right about finding a place for us to sprawl luxuriously.

Then I remembered that Uncle had willed his house to Sachish. If the will had been with Sachish it would have sunk like a paper boat in the waves of his ecstatic devotion. But it was with me; I was the executor. My task was to ensure the fulfilment of certain conditions, of which the most important were: that no religious service could be held in the house; that a night school for the children of the Muslim tanners had to be set up on the ground floor; and that after Sachish's death the whole house had to be used for their welfare. Uncle hated piety more than anything else and considered it more vile than worldliness. The provisions in the will were intended to neutralize the odour of sanctity from next door. Uncle described them – using the English term – as 'sanitary precautions'.

'Let's go back to Uncle's house in Calcutta,' I suggested to Sachish.

'I am not yet ready for that,' Sachish replied.

I couldn't see what he meant. He went on: 'Once I tried to base my life on intelligence and found that it couldn't take life's full weight. Then I tried to build my life on ecstatic devotion and found it was bottomless. Intelligence is an aspect of my self, and so is mysticism. It is not possible to balance oneself on oneself. Unless I find some support I can't return to the city.'

'Tell me what to do,' I said.

'You two go ahead,' Sachish said. 'I'll wander alone for a while. I think I can make out the vague outline of a shore. If I lose it now I'll never find it again.'

Damini drew me aside and said, 'That cannot be. If he wanders all by himself who will look after him? He did go away once. I shudder whenever I remember how he looked when he came back.'

Shall I confess the truth? Damini's anxiety roused me into anger like a bee-sting. It irked me. For nearly two years after Uncle's death Sachish had wandered alone; he hadn't died. I couldn't suppress my feelings and I spoke out pungently.

'Sribilashbabu,' Damini said, 'I know people may take long to die. But why should he suffer at all when we are there?'

We! At least half of the first-person plural was this wretched Sribilash. In this world one group of people has to suffer in order to save another group from distress. The world of *samsara* is made up of these two categories of human beings. Damini well knew to which group I belonged. Still, it was some consolation that she had drawn me into her party.

I went to Sachish and said, 'Very well, we won't go to the city now. We can spend a few days in that ruined house across the river. Since it's rumoured to be haunted, people won't bother you there.'

'And you?' Sachish asked.

'We'll try to remain as unobtrusive as ghosts,' I said.

Sachish glanced once at Damini. Perhaps there was a touch of fear in that glance.

Damini appealed to Sachish with joined palms, 'You are my guru. No matter how greatly I may sin, allow me the right to serve you.'

2

Whatever you may say, I couldn't understand Sachish's enthusiasm for spiritual austerities. Once I would have dismissed such things with a laugh; now – whatever else – my laughter had ceased. I was dealing no longer with a will-o'-the-wisp, but with a blazing fire. When I saw its flames engulf Sachish I didn't dare behave towards it like a disciple of Uncle's. What phantasmagoric faith gave birth to it and what miraculous faith would ultimately consume it? It was pointless to approach Mr. Herbert Spencer to settle such questions. I could clearly see that Sachish was in flames, his life was ablaze from end to end.

Until now he had been in a state of perpetual excitement, singing and dancing, shedding tears of joy, attending on his guru; and in a way he was quite content. His mind was exerted to the utmost at every moment, squandering all his energy. Now that he had gathered himself in stillness, his mind could no longer be kept in check. No more did he wallow in mystic contemplation of ecstatic union with the divine. Such a desperate struggle to attain understanding raged within him that it was terrifying to look upon his face.

Unable to contain myself any longer I said to him one day, 'Look here, Sachish, it seems to me you need a guru who can lend you the support to make your quest easier.'

'O shut up, Bisri, shut up,' Sachish replied with annoyance, 'why take the easy way out? The easy way is a fraud, the truth is hard to attain.'

I said a little nervously, 'It is in order to show the way to the truth that . . .'

Sachish cut me short: 'My fear fellow, this isn't the truth of a geographical description. The god within me will tread my road and none other; the guru's road only leads to his own courtyard.'

Words from Sachish's lips have so often contradicted each other! I, Sribilash, was Uncle's follower no doubt, but if I had ever called him my guru he would have chased me with a stick. Sachish had got me, the selfsame Sribilash, to massage a guru's legs, and now soon after he was giving this lecture to the very same me! Not daring to laugh, I adopted a sombre expression.

Sachish went on. 'Today I have clearly grasped the significance of the saying, "Better die for one's own faith than do such a terrible thing as accept another's." Everything else can be taken from others, but if one's faith isn't one's own it brings damnation instead of salvation. My god can't be doled out to me by someone; if I find him, well and good, otherwise it's better to die.'

I am contentious by nature, not one to let go easily. 'One who is a poet finds poetry in his soul,' I said, 'and one who isn't borrows it from others.'

'I am a poet,' said Sachish brazenly.

Well, that settled it. I came away.

Sachish hardly bothered to eat or sleep and seemed oblivious of his whereabouts. His body seemed to grow as thin as an over-honed blade. Looking at him one would think he wouldn't hold out much longer. Still, I didn't dare interfere. But Damini couldn't bear it and became quite furious with God: frustrated by those who didn't worship him, must he take it out on those who did? With Swami Lilananda she could occasionally vent her rage quite forcefully, but there was no chance of reaching God.

She never, though, slackened her efforts to keep Sachish fed and bathed regularly. To bind this strange man to a routine, she resorted to countless ruses.

For a long time Sachish made no protest against this. Then early one morning he crossed the river to the sand flats on the other side. The sun reached its zenith, then declined to the west, but there was no sign of Sachish. Damini waited for him without eating her meal. When she could no longer bear the wait she took a plate laden with food and waded across the knee-deep water.

Emptiness all around, no sign of life anywhere. The waves of sand were as pitiless as the sun – as if they were sentinels of emptiness, lying in ambush.

Damini's heart sank as she stood in the middle of an unbounded, bleached space where no cry or query drew any response. Everything seemed to have dissolved into primal dry whiteness. There was nothing at her feet save a 'No' – no sound or motion, no trace of the red of blood, the green of plants, the blue of the sky or the brown of earth. Only the wide, lipless grin of a gigantic death's-head. As if under the pitiless blazing sky a huge dry tongue was displaying its thirst like a vast petition.

Damini was wondering which way to turn when she suddenly noticed footprints in the sand. Following them she reached a pond. The wet earth of its edges bore innumerable footprints of birds. Sachish was seated in the shade cast by a sandbank. The water was dazzling blue and on the bank fidgety snipes dipped their tails and flashed their two-tone wings. A little farther off noisy flocks of herons seemed unable to preen themselves to their satisfaction. As soon as Damini appeared on the bank they spread wings and took off with loud squawks.

When he saw her Sachish said, 'Why are you here?'

'I've brought some food,' Damini replied.

'I don't want to eat,' Sachish said.

'It's very late,' said Damini.

Sachish just said, 'No.'

Damini went on. 'Let me wait a little. After a while you . . .'

Sachish cut in. 'Oh, why do you . . .'

But suddenly catching sight of Damini's face he stopped. Without another word Damini got up with the plate and left. The bare sand all around glittered like tigers' eyes at night.

Damini's eyes blazed more readily than they shed tears. But that day I found her squatting with legs carelessly splayed while tears streamed from her eyes. On seeing me, her sobs seemed to burst through a dam. My heart felt uneasy. I sat down beside her.

When she had composed herself somewhat I said, 'Why do you worry so much about Sachish's health?'

Tell me,' she replied, 'what else can I worry about? He has taken all other worries on himself. Do I understand them or do anything about them?'

'Look,' I said, 'when the mind runs hard into something the body's needs automatically diminish. That's why in a state of great joy or intense grief one feels no hunger or thirst. Sachish's state of mind is such that his body won't suffer if you don't look after it.'

'But I am a woman,' Damini protested. 'It is in our nature to devote ourselves body and soul to caring for the body. This task is entirely the responsibility of women. That's why when we see the body being neglected our hearts cry out.'

'That's why those who are preoccupied with their spirits don't even notice guardians of the body like you,' I said.

Damini retorted warmly, 'Don't they indeed! In fact they take notice in a way that's quite weird.'

'In that case,' I said to myself, 'the longing of your sex for the weird is boundless . . . O Sribilash, earn enough merit in this world so that you can be reborn as one of those weirdos.'

3

The outcome of the shock Sachish dealt Damini on the riverbank was that he couldn't erase from his memory her anxious expression as she had gone up to him. For some days after he did penance by paying special attention to Damini. For a long time he hadn't even bothered to speak politely with us; now he would often call Damini for a chat. They talked about the results of his profound meditation.

Damini had not been afraid of Sachish's indifference, but these attentions filled her with dread. She knew they were too good to last, for they came at a price. One day he would look at the balance sheet and see that the expenditure was too high. Then there would be trouble. Damini's heart trembled in apprehension, a strange embarrassment overcame her when Sachish behaved like an obedient child and had his bath and meals at regular hours. She would have felt relieved if he had disobeyed the rules. She said to herself, 'He did right to spurn me that day. But by paying me attention now he is only punishing himself. How can I bear that?' Then she thought: 'Damn it all. It seems that in this place also I'll have to make friends with the local women and spend time hanging around the village.'

One night we were woken up by loud shouts: 'Bisri! Damini!' It was one or two in the morning but Sachish would have no inkling of that. What he might be up to at such an hour I didn't know, but clearly his activities were driving the ghostly denizens of that haunted house to distraction.

We got up in a hurry and went out to find Sachish standing on the cement terrace in front of the house. 'I understand it all,' he shouted. 'There's no more doubt in my mind.'

Slowly Damini sat down on the terrace. Sachish followed her absent-mindedly and sat down. So did I.

'If,' Sachish said, 'I move in the same direction in which He is approaching me I'll only move away from Him, but if I move in the opposite direction we shall meet.'

I stared in silence at his burning eyes. What he had said was correct according to linear geometry, but what was it all about?

Sachish continued. 'He loves form, so He is continuously revealing Himself through form. We can't survive with form alone, so we must pursue the formless. He is free, so he delights in bondage; we are fettered, so our joy is in liberty. Our misery arises because we don't realize this truth.'

Damini and I remained as silent as the stars. 'Damini,' Sachish said, 'don't you understand? The singer progresses from the experience of joy to the musical expression of the *raga*, the audience in the opposite direction from the *raga* towards joy. One moves from freedom to bondage, the other from bondage to freedom; hence the concord between them. He sings, we listen. He plays by binding emotion to the *raga* and as we listen we unravel the emotion from the *raga*.'

I don't know whether Damini understood what Sachish was saying, but she did understand Sachish. She sat quietly, hands folded in her lap.

'All this while,' Sachish said, 'I've been sitting in a dark corner, listening in silence to the divine maestro's song. As I went on listening I suddenly understood everything. I couldn't contain myself, so I woke you up. All these days I've only fooled myself in trying to make Him in my own image. O my apocalypse, let me forever crush myself against you! I can't cling to any bondage because bondage isn't mine, and because bondage is yours you can never escape the fetters of creation. While you concern yourself with my form I plunge into your formlessness.'

Then saying over and over the words, 'O Infinity, you are mine, you are mine,' Sachish got up and walked through the dark towards the riverbank.

4

After that night Sachish reverted to his former ways. There was no knowing when he would bathe or eat. It was impossible to make out when the currents of his soul sought the light, or when they sought darkness. Whoever takes on the responsibility of keeping such a person regularly bathed and fed like a gentleman's son deserves divine assistance.

After a sultry day a violent storm burst at night. The three of us slept in separate rooms fronting a veranda on which a naked kerosene lamp burned. It went out. The river surged, the sky burst into torrents of rain. The thrashing of the waves below and the noise of the rain in the sky mingled to produce the continuous cymbal-crashes of an apocalyptic concert. We could see nothing of the turbulence within the womb of the massed darkness, yet the medley of noises emanating from it turned the entire sky as cold with fright as a blind child. A widowed ghoul seemed to shriek in the bamboo thickets, branches groaned and crashed in the mango grove, intermittently in the distance portions of the riverbank collapsed thunderously into the water, and as the gale repeatedly stabbed our dilapidated house with sharp thrusts through the ribs it howled like a wounded beast.

On a night like this the bolts to the doors and windows of the mind come loose, the storm enters and upsets the carefully arranged furniture, the curtains flap and flutter any which way and there's no catching hold of them. I couldn't sleep. There's no point transcribing the random thoughts that passed through my mind; they have no relevance to the story.

Suddenly I heard Sachish shout from within his dark room: 'Who is it?'

'It's Damini,' came the reply. 'The rain is getting in through your open window. I've come to shut it.'

As she did so she saw Sachish get out of bed. After what appeared to be momentary hesitation he bolted out of the room. Lightning flashed, followed by a muffled rumble of thunder.

Damini sat for a long time in the doorway of her own room. But nobody came in from the storm. The gusty wind grew more and more impatient.

Unable to restrain herself any longer, Damini went out. It was hard to keep one's balance in the wind. Footmen of the gods hustled her along, as it were, with loud imprecations. The darkness began to stir. The rain tried desperately to fill all the holes and crannies in the sky. If only she herself could have deluged the cosmos like this with her tears.

Suddenly a lightning shaft ripped through the sky from end to end. In the fleeting light Damini spotted Sachish on the riverbank. Mustering all her strength she ran and fell at his feet. Her voice triumphed over the wind's roar as she begged, 'I swear at your feet that I have not wronged you, so why do you punish me like this?'

Sachish stood in silence.

'Kick me into the river if you wish,' Damini said, 'but get out of the storm.'

Sachish turned back. As soon as he got back to the house he said, 'I am seeking a Being whom I need desperately. I don't need anything else. Do me a favour, Damini. Abandon me.'

For a while Damini stood in silence. Then she said, 'Very well, I'll go.'

5

Later I heard the whole story from Damini, but that day I knew nothing of it. And so when from my bed I saw the two of them part on the front veranda and walk to their respective rooms, my hopelessness seemed to crush my chest and reach for my throat. I sat up in a panic and couldn't go back to sleep all night.

I was shocked at Damini's appearance the next morning. Last night's storm seemed to have left on her all the footprints of its dance of destruction. Though ignorant of what had transpired I began to feel angry with Sachish.

'Come, Sribilashbabu,' Damini said to me, 'you will have to escort me to Calcutta.'

I knew very well what agony such words were for Damini but I didn't probe her with questions. Even in the midst of anguish I experienced a sense of relief. It was for the best that Damini should leave. She was like a boat that had wrecked itself against a rock.

At the leave-taking Damini bowed to Sachish in a *pranam* and said, 'I have offended you in many ways. Please forgive me.'

Lowering his gaze to the ground Sachish said, 'I have also done much wrong. I will do penance to obtain forgiveness.'

On the way to Calcutta I saw clearly that Damini was being consumed by an apocalyptic inferno. And I too – inflamed to fury by its heat – said some harsh things about Sachish. 'Look here,' Damini shot back, 'don't you talk like that about him in my presence. Have you any idea of what he has saved me from? You have eyes for my suffering only. Can't you see how *he* has suffered in order to save me? He tried to destroy Beauty, and in the process the Unbeautiful got a kick in the chest. Just as well . . . just as well . . . it was quite right.' Saying this Damini began violently striking her chest. I caught hold of her wrists.

On reaching Calcutta I took Damini to her aunt's, then went to a boarding-house I knew. On seeing me my acquaintances were startled into exclaiming, 'What on earth's the matter with you? Have you been ill?'

The following day the first post brought a note from Damini: 'Please take me away. I am not wanted here.'

The aunt wouldn't let Damini live with her. The city was apparently buzzing with condemnation of us. Shortly after our desertion of the guru's party the *Puja* specials of the weeklies came out; so the chopping blocks were ready for us, and there was no dearth of bloodshed. The scriptures forbid the sacrifice of female animals, but in the case of human beings sacrificing females gives the greatest satisfaction. Though Damini's name was not explicitly mentioned in the papers care was taken to ensure that there would be no doubt about the target of the slander. Consequently it became totally impossible for Damini to live in her aunt's house.

By now Damini's parents were both dead. Her brothers, however, were still around. I asked her about their whereabouts. 'They are very poor,' she said with a shake of her head.

The fact was she didn't want to put them in a difficult position. She feared that the brothers too would say, 'No room for you here!' The blow would be unbearable. 'So where will you go?' I asked.

'To Swami Lilananda.'

Swami Lilananda! I was struck dumb for a while. Fortune could be so cruelly whimsical!

'Will Swamiji take you back?' I asked.

'Gladly.'

She knew human nature. Those dominated by the herd instinct prefer to find company than to seek truth. It was quite true that there would be no lack of room for Damini at Swami Lilananda's. Still . . .

At this critical moment I said, 'Damini, there's a way out. If you'll permit me I'll explain.'

'Let's hear,' Damini said.

'If it's possible for you to accept a man like me in marriage . . .'

Damini interrupted me. 'What are you saying, Sribilashbabu? Have you gone mad?'

'Let's say I have. When you're mad it becomes easy to solve many difficult problems. Madness is a pair of Arabian Nights shoes; if you put them on you can leap clear of thousands of bogus questions.'

'Bogus questions? What exactly do you mean by bogus?'

'For instance, what will people say? What will happen in future?'

'And the real questions?' Damini asked.

'Let's hear what you understand by real questions.'

'For instance, what will happen to you if you marry me?'

'If that's the real question I'm not worried, because my condition can't get worse. If only I could change it completely. Even turning it over on its side would provide a little relief.'

I refuse to believe that Damini had not already received some sort of telepathic message about my feelings. But till now this information had been of no consequence to her; or at least there had been no need for a reply. Now at last the need had arisen.

Damini pondered the matter in silence. 'Damini,' I said, 'I am one of the most ordinary men in this world. Indeed, I am less than that, I am insignificant. Marrying me or not marrying me will make no difference, so you needn't worry.'

Damini's eyes brimmed over. 'I wouldn't have to consider it at all if you were really ordinary,' she said.

After a little more thought Damini said to me, 'Well, you know me.'

'You know me too,' I said.

That is how I put my proposal. In the exchange between us the unspoken words outnumbered the spoken.

I have already mentioned that I had once conquered many hearts with my orations in English. In the time that had elapsed many had shaken off the spell. But Naren still regarded me as one of God's gifts to the present age. A house he owned was to remain untenanted for a month or so. We took temporary shelter there.

The day I put the question to Damini the wheels of my proposal had buckled and run into such a rut of silence that it seemed it would remain stuck there, beyond the reach of both 'yes' and 'no'. If only with extensive repairs and much hauling and heaving I could get it out! But the situation was unexpectedly saved because the psyche has been created – perhaps as a jest – specially to deceive the psychologist. That spring month of Phalgun, the

Creator's merry laughter over this reverberated between the walls of our borrowed quarters.

All these days Damini had not had the time to recognize that I was of any consequence; perhaps a more intense light from another source was entering her eyes. Now her whole world narrowed to a point where I was the sole presence. Consequently there was nothing for her to do but open her eyes wide to see me. How lucky I was that just at this moment Damini seemed to see me for the first time.

I had roamed widely in Damini's company, by the sea and across many hills and rivers, while ecstatic melodies and a tumult of drums and cymbals set the air on fire. The line, 'At your footsteps the noose of love tightens round my soul,' was like a flame showering sparks in all directions. Yet the veil between us didn't catch fire.

But what an extraordinary thing happened in this Calcutta alley! The jostling houses seemed to turn into blossoms of amaranth. Truly, God gave a spectacular demonstration of his powers. Brick and woodwork became notes in his celestial melody. And with the touch of a philosopher's stone of some kind he instantly transformed a nonentity like me into an exceptional being.

When something is concealed behind a screen it seems eternally inaccessible, but when the screen is removed it can be reached in the twinkling of an eye. So we didn't tarry any longer. 'I was living in a dream,' Damini said. 'All I needed was to be jolted awake. A veil of illusion kept us separate. I bow to my guru in gratitude, for he removed the veil.'

'Don't stare at me like that,' I said to Damini. 'When you once before found that this particular divine creation wasn't attractive, I could bear it, but it would be very difficult to bear it now.'

'I'm now finding that same creation to be quite good-looking,' Damini said.

'You'll go down in history,' I said. 'Even the fame of the intrepid man who plants his flag at the North Pole will be nothing compared to yours. You have achieved something not merely difficult, but impossible.'

Never before did I have such an absolute realization of the extreme brevity of Phalgun. Only thirty days, and each of them not a minute longer than twenty-four hours. God has all eternity in his hands, and yet such appalling niggardliness! I couldn't see why.

'Since setting yourself on this mad course, have you thought of your family?' Damini asked.

'They wish me well,' I said. 'So now they will disown me completely.'

'And then?'

'You and I will build a new home from scratch. It will be our very own creation.'

'And the housewife in it will have to be trained from scratch. Let her be entirely your own creation, let there be no fragments of the past.'

We set a date for our wedding in the summer month of Chaitra, and made the necessary arrangements. Damini insisted on getting Sachish to come.

'Why?' I asked.

'He will give away the bride.'

But there was no news of the madcap's whereabouts. I wrote letter after letter and got no reply. Probably he was still at that haunted house; otherwise the letters would have come back. But I doubted whether he opened any letter and read it.

'Damini,' I said, 'you'll have to convey the invitation in person. "Please forgive an invitation by post" – that sort of thing won't do here. I could have gone alone, but I am a timid sort of fellow. By now he has probably moved to the other side of the river to supervise the herons at their preening. Only you would have the guts to go there.'

'I promised never to go there again,' Damini said with a laugh.

'You promised not to go there again with food, but what's the harm in taking an invitation to a meal?' I said.

This time there was no hitch. The two of us took Sachish by the hand and marched him back to Calcutta. He was as delighted over our wedding as a child is with a new toy. We wanted to get it over with quietly; Sachish would have none of that. And when Uncle's

Muslim following got wind of the event, they gave themselves up to such boisterous revelry that our neighbours thought the Emir of Kabul – or at least the Nizam of Hyderabad – had arrived on a ceremonial visit.

There was even greater excitement in the papers. The next *Puja* specials duly provided the altar for a dual sacrifice. We have no desire to put a curse on anybody, though. Let Durga fill the coffers of the editors and at least this once let readers freely indulge their addiction to human blood.

'Bisri, I'd like you to use my house,' Sachish said.

'Why don't you join us too, so that we can get to work again?' I replied.

'No, my work lies elsewhere,' Sachish said.

'You can't leave before the *bou-bhat* ceremony,' Damini insisted.

There weren't too many guests at the *bou-bhat*. In fact there was only Sachish.

Sachish had blithely invited us to enjoy the use of his property, but what it entailed only we knew. Harimohan had taken possession of it and rented it out. He would have moved in himself, but those who advised him on spiritual matters considered it unwise because some Muslims had died of the plague there. The tenants who lived there would also . . . But they could be kept in the dark.

How we retrieved the house from Harimohan's grip would make a long tale. Our chief strength lay in the neighbourhood Muslims. I simply gave them a glimpse of Jagmohan's will. After that it was unnecessary to go to any lawyer.

Till now I had always received some help from my family; it stopped. The two of us set up house unaided, but our hardship was our delight. I bore the badge of a Premchand-Raychand scholar, so it was easy to land a lectureship. In addition I put out patent medicines to help students pass examinations: voluminous notes on the text-books. I needn't have gone to such lengths, because our needs were few. But Damini said we must see to it that Sachish didn't have to worry about earning a living. There was another thing Damini didn't ask me to do, nor did I speak to her about it; it had to be done on the quiet. Damini's brothers lacked the means to ensure that her two nieces were married well or her several nephews well educated. They wouldn't let us into their houses – but money has no smell, especially when it merely has to be accepted and needn't be acknowledged.

On top of my other responsibilities I took up the sub-editorship of an English newspaper. Without telling Damini I engaged the services of a servant-boy, a bearer and an indigent Brahmin cook. The next day she dismissed them all without telling me. When I objected she said, 'You are always indulging me for the wrong reasons. How on earth can I do nothing while you are working yourself to the bone?'

My work outside and Damini's work inside the home – the two mingled like the confluence of the Ganges and the Jamuna. Besides, Damini began giving sewing lessons to the Muslim girls of the neighbourhood. She seemed to have vowed not to be outdone by me.

Calcutta became Brindaban and our daily struggle became the nimble Krishna's flute, but I lack the poetic talent to express this simple truth in the right key. Let me just say that the days that went by didn't walk or run, they danced.

We passed yet another Phalgun. But no more after that. Ever since the return from the cave Damini had been suffering from a pain in the chest that she mentioned to no one. When it began getting worse she said in reply to my anxious queries: 'This pain is my secret glory, my philosopher's stone. It is the dowry that enabled me to come to you, otherwise I wouldn't have deserved you.'

The doctors each diagnosed the ailment differently. None of their prescriptions agreed. Eventually, when like Rama conquering Lanka the blaze of their fees and medicine bills had reduced my savings to cinders, the doctors capped their triumph by pronouncing unanimously that a change of air was necessary. By then my resources had dwindled into air.

'Take me to the place by the sea from where I brought the pain,' Damini said. 'There's plenty of air there.'

When the full moon of wintry Magh gave way to Phalgun and the entire sea rose, filled with the aching tears of high tide, Damini took the dust of my feet and said, 'My longings are still with me. I go with the prayer that I may find you again in my next life.'

Glossary

Airavata   the white elephant, created by the churning of the ocean; became the mount of the god Indra

akanda   mauve flower growing on a small tree

Ashar   the first of the two months of the rainy season, mid-June to mid-July

baba   father; also used affectionately for a son or young boy

babu   a gentleman; as a suffix added to a name it is equivalent to 'Mister', e.g. Sribilashbabu

bhantiphool   sweet-smelling white flower with deep red spots

bou-bhat   *bou* means bride, *bhat* rice. One of the many traditional Hindu wedding feasts, organized by the groom's family to welcome the bride

Chaitra   the second of the two spring months in the Bengali calendar, mid-March to mid-April; it is hot and dry

chalta   an evergreen tree bearing large white scented blossoms and an edible fruit

chamar   traditionally the caste of leather-workers, described as 'untouchable'

dada   elder brother, grandfather, great-uncle

Durga   one of the fierce forms assumed by the great Hindu goddess Devi, when she is the great protectress of humanity

Hladini, *Sandhini* and *Jogmaya*   all associated with Vaishnava cults based on the ideal love of Radha and Krishna as the path to the realization of the Ultimate Being. Hladini, identified with Radha, manifests the power of bliss; Sandhini, the power of existence; Jogmaya, identified with Durga, the power of divine diffusion

jap   the silent recitation of prayers and mantras

ji   suffix added to a name or title as a mark of respect, e.g. Swamiji

kaystha   important high caste of North India, originally of scribes

khichuri   dish of rice cooked with *dal* (pulses)

kirtan   religious songs celebrating sacred romance of Krishna and Radha

kulin   the highest subcaste of Brahmins, traditionally said to have been created by the twelfth-century Bengal king, Sena

Lanka   ancient name of Sri Lanka

Ma   mother; used affectionately for a daughter or young woman

Magh   the second of the two winter months in the Bengali calendar, mid-January to mid-February

Manu   orthodox Hindu law-giver, probably legendary

maya   illusion; the mundane realm, considered illustory in relation to the (transcendental) ultimate reality

namaskar   the Hindu salute, given by bowing (*nama*) and simultaneously raising joined palms

pan   betel-leaf filled with various spices, chewed as a digestive

Phalgun   the first of the two spring months in the Bengali calendar, mid-February to mid-March

pranam   obeisance made by kneeling and touching forehead to the floor

puja   Hindu worship; often used as a shorthand for Durga Puja, the chief festival of Bengali Hindus, when magazines and periodicals publish special numbers

Puranas   Hindu ancient narratives with a didactic purpose about the birth and deeds of gods and goddesses and mythological characters

raga   Indian musical mode, e.g. *raga shahana*, mentioned in the novella

rasa   generally translated here as 'ecstasy'. It is a key concept in Sanskrit aesthetics as 'mood', of which there are nine principal ones: erotic, comic, compassionate, heroic, terrible, disgusting, wrathful, wonderful, calm. A work of art evokes one or more. In ordinary parlance it means the sap/essence/juice of life. In colloquial Bengali it can mean the sex drive

samsara   the world of the householder, characterized by worldly attachments

sannyasi   one who has renounced the world; a religious mendicant

sannyasini   feminine form of *sannyasi*

sissoo   large deciduous tree, valuable for its timber

sraddha   rituals and feast marking the end of the period of mourning among Hindus

tikka   cake of charcoal paste used as fuel to light the tobacco in the tobacco-bowl of a hookah

Ucchaisraba   the horse of the god Indra

Veena   ancient stringed musical instrument, used chiefly in classical music